Totally Bound Publishing books by Sandra Carmel

I0680900

Oh, Baby

THE BEST-LAID PLANS

SANDRA CARMEL

The Best-Laid Plans
ISBN # 978-1-80250-773-7
©Copyright Sandra Carmel 2024
Cover Art by Kelly Martin ©Copyright July 2024
Interior text design by Claire Siemaszkiewicz
Totally Bound Publishing

Published in 2024 by Totally Bound Publishing, United Kingdom.

THE BEST-LAID PLANS

Dedication

For those of you who have successfully
surmounted the challenges of love.

Chapter One

"What do you mean? This is bullshit!" Archer Aldrich stomped across the expansive floor of his plush office and stared through the window at the gridlocked traffic below — the new norm in Melbourne's central business district.

His great-uncle Salvator had died in 2011. *Fucking twelve years ago.* And until Archer's grandma passed away recently, he'd had no idea about the guy's will. Fuck, he hadn't even been eligible to inherit until now. Apparently those before him had failed to meet the stipulations, and he was the next — and last — in line.

"Maybe, but legally, I can't do anything about it. The only way for you to receive your full entitlement is to find a wife...and the sooner, the financially more viable. The conditions state you need to marry before Valentine's Day."

What the fuck? How could his solicitor sound so matter-of-fact, so calm? How could he not think the whole thing was irrational? Ludicrous. Overly sickly saccharine. A total dreamer's mentality. The fucking stats, the data, showed that one in two marriages ended in divorce.

So if not for some stupid will proviso, what drove people down the committed monogamy path? Why bother searching for a supposedly special needle in a stack of similar needles?

Made absolutely no sense. There were so many attractive, available women. Why settle for only one? "Come on. There has to be some way to break such a ridiculous, outdated requirement."

"Unfortunately not. Believe me, I've investigated all options, and I can't supersede the soulmate clause."

Archer massaged his forehead with firm, inflexible fingers. What was with his great-uncle? The guy had become so obsessed with soulmates he'd even developed a serum to determine whether someone was a person's fated life partner. Could he *really* be related to Salvator? Their beliefs were practically polar opposites.

Who fucking cared about finding 'the one'? Why not enjoy every individual partner for their contribution to each unique experience. "So…what? I need to find a woman I like and marry her before the fourteenth of February? That's only a few months away." He huffed. "And if I don't?"

"You receive a small consolatory amount, and the bulk of the money goes to the Jade and Violet Vampire Foundation to support health and wellbeing in the vampire community."

Archer swore under his breath, frustrated as all fuck. "You have to be kidding me. Salvator didn't even have any vampire genetics!"

"Would I joke about something like this?"

No, the guy wouldn't. He had nothing to gain. But Archer did. A whole fucking huge stash of cash. The way Salvator had invested, it would set him up for the rest of his life. Hell, extend way beyond it.

He'd be a total fuckhead if he looked this unconventional gift horse in the mouth. "Fine. You'll be the first to hear about my engagement." Archer stabbed his index finger at the red 'end call' button, and threw his phone onto the desk.

Fuck, he didn't even have a love interest, a regular date. Didn't even believe in the institution of marriage. And the festive season had already started with no female prospects.

The countdown to Christmas had commenced, leaving just a measly few months to not only find an agreeable woman but also convince her to marry him.

No pressure. Yeah. He dropped into his office chair, his head in his hands. Like he fucking needed this extra stress... Like it wasn't already a massive pain in the ass ensuring his company made a profit while ignoring the unexplainable attraction he had to his Norwegian business partner's sexy sister...

Not conventionally sexy. Sort of sexy in a nerdy way. Not normally his type, but something about her got him going. Probably her hybrid vampire genetics. Probably the forbidden aspect. Probably the fact that he couldn't have her, even though every one of her actions screamed for a Dominant's direction. *His* direction.

Archer normally couldn't resist a challenge, but in this instance, he had to. He couldn't hook up with his friend's sweet sister unless he aimed for more of a future. He couldn't screw her over — not that he'd plan to, but shit happened — or his business partner buddy, to satisfy a short-term need.

His cock disagreed, desperate to sink into her wet heat. But he couldn't take advantage. *No fucking way.*

That would break the 'bro' business code, as well as his strong scrupulous stance.

He might have a history of changing women more often than he changed his underwear, but every relationship he entered into was one hundred percent consensual. No matter what people believed, he did have an honorable bone in his body.

Did he struggle to accept the restrictive circumstances? Ignore his Neanderthal needs? Fuck, yes. Ever since Temperance Elskelig had arrived in Melbourne on a working visa, he'd had an extremely hard time resisting the woman.

But he refused to cross the lustful line, despite how often his sinful side begged him to have her just once. If he did give in to his impulses, his whole life could come crashing down around him like persistent, pelting rockfall, burying him under an avalanche of regret. The roll-on effect destroying her, too.

Wrong.

So fucking wrong and supremely selfish.

Although he wanted her on a primal level, acknowledged it, he couldn't lead her on or pretend he could offer her forever, when he had never even shown a propensity for staying the night after a hookup. Had never had a long-term relationship…unless a couple of weeks met the criteria.

Yeah…no.

A knock sounded on his office door. "Archer? Are you available?"

Not usually, but for Temperance, the woman in question…? Her sweet, melodic voice penetrated the timber and touched a spot deep within him, right in the vicinity of his usually impenetrable heart.

His principles ensured his conquests clearly understood his intentions, but until her, no one had ever broken the lust barrier.

Did she have ESP? Had she tuned in to his complicated thoughts? Everyone knew that those with vampire genetics often had special powers.

"Come in." If only he could.

Enough.

Time to dial back the debauchery and switch into professional boss mode.

Temperance eased the door open and stepped inside, a nervous smile tugging at the corners of her luscious lips. She avoided eye contact, as usual, her long, wavy bronze hair framing her beautiful face.

If she didn't know it already, she qualified as the quintessential submissive, another endearing trait he couldn't ignore. It spoke right to his inner Dom.

His cock agreed, saluting her stunning presence. And thankfully, although painfully, it remained confined in his suddenly too-tight pants. Having her so close, in his space, his lust-o-meter practically redlined. He wanted to forget protocol, forget sensibility, stride over to the temptress and slam his mouth onto hers.

He'd lost count of how many times he'd masturbated before bed, imagining her bound and gagged and on display for his pleasure…and hers, because a huge part of him getting off relied on pleasing his partner. No, not purely pleasing — taking her right to the outer extremes of ecstasy.

"Sir, I have the reports you requested." Her use of *Sir*, combined with her Scandinavian accent sent a surge of desire directly to his dick. She stumbled across the room and deposited said reports on his desk. Averted eyes, shaky hands, soft voice. Sexy as fuck.

Sir. How he wanted her to address him in that way outside of work. In the back of his car, on his couch, on his kitchen bench, in his bedroom, in the spa — over and over and over.

Stop it.

He had to rein in his thinking before he lost all sense of decorum and acted on his overpowering urges. "You could have emailed them." His voice came out choppy, abrupt, strangled.

"I've done that, too. With your meeting this afternoon, I thought you might want a hard copy to review prior, to make notes on and highlight any relevant sections."

How could someone be so fucking smart, innocent and sexy all in one irresistible package? He forced himself to stay behind his desk and gripped tight to the last vestiges of his usually ironclad control. "Thank you."

She glanced at him — the first time their eyes had met since she'd entered the room and, fuck, did they pack a powerful punch — her forehead furrowed as though shocked. Had he gone too hardass, alpha boss-hole in the past, in an attempt to keep her beyond arm's length? Been too gruff, brash, hardcore Dom?

Shit, yeah. He'd done whatever he could so she, and her brother, had not even the tiniest hint of his attraction to her.

She shifted from foot to foot and studied her now-empty hands as though they were the most interesting things she'd ever observed. "Um, do you need anything else?"

Aside from her straddling his lap and him kissing her senseless? Driving his dick deep between her gorgeous legs and fucking her until she screamed his name?

"Not at the moment. Thanks." His curt, dismissive 'me-master, you-servant' tone had her racing to exit his office like she couldn't wait to escape.

Had he scared her? Been too intimidating? *Most likely.* People had given him that feedback many times over the years, plus added a few other choice words. But he didn't want her to think of him as aloof or arrogant, or to instill fear in the sweet little sub. He craved her respect. A massive difference.

Archer pushed out of his office chair, headed to the coffee-pod machine in his mini bar and took his freshly made macchiato to the window. Cars still sat bumper-to-bumper, but some movement had returned.

What a fucking day. First the weird-ass will criteria, then the Temperance temptation. He needed to stop fixating on her and her unavailability and focus on finding a fake wife — at least until he met the full terms of his inheritance. Someone he liked who'd agree to a short-term, paid arrangement, preferably with perks.

Yeah, okay, it sounded crass and cheap, but not with the right person. Ideally he'd choose someone who, like him, had their own agenda, which included having fun as part of the deal.

But who in his regular social circle met that criterion? He had a sip of his coffee. *Rich, full-bodied, aromatic. Fucking perfect.* His mind searched through candidates...

It had to be someone who wouldn't want more. Would accept the need-to-be-wed-by-Valentine's-Day terms, preferably stay married for at least a few weeks and play along, knowing he'd remunerate them. The woman would receive a healthy sum of money to successfully set up her own life. He wouldn't offer anything less.

She'd be handsomely compensated for a scant few months of her time. He sifted through his back catalog of feasible female contacts. Who could he trust to not only agree to the terms but also ensure the curious cat didn't flee from the flimsy bag?

An extensive history of women paraded through his head. *No, no, no, no, no.* He grabbed his mobile phone off the desk and scrolled through his long list of friends-with-benefits. Maybe he'd missed someone?

Nope.

Archer couldn't imagine spending longer than a few nights in one hit, let alone several months with any of them. Hence why they'd been relegated to past flings or occasional hook-ups, and he was still single.

Man, he was fucked. So fucked. Not one woman stood out in his mind, except the one he couldn't have.

Temperance.

Normally he loved the chance to overcome adversity, loved to tackle and conquer whatever he, or others, believed he couldn't do. It developed strength of character and positive forward movement.

However, the Temperance situation was a fuck-ton more complicated.

He blew out a frustrated breath, dropped his phone back on the desk and ran his fingers through his hair.

His mobile buzzed, his business partner's face filling the screen. Bror, Temperance's brother. What fucked-up timing? Had the guy sensed something? Was he another hybrid with special powers? One way to find out for sure.

He answered the video call on the fourth ring. "Hey, mate, what can I do you for?"

"I have a favor to ask." The guy had an unblinking stare that would scare the fuck out of most people, but not Archer. He'd known Bror for years. They'd met at a business conference in America and had kept in touch, their close friendship morphing into a collective enterprise.

It hadn't taken long for Archer to determine the difference between when the guy wanted to discuss something serious or was truly pissed off.

"Go ahead." Hopefully he'd read him accurately and the guy's request wouldn't make his day any more difficult.

"Temperance needs a husband."

What? And he was asking him because? "Why?" Archer focused on keeping his expression curious yet neutral.

"To get fast-tracked approval for a permanent visa. Do you know someone…suitable?"

What the fuck did *suitable* mean? A good guy, a hybrid, a full Jade or Violet? Didn't make a difference. Not to him. "No." No fucking way. He wouldn't let any of the single guys he knew touch her, whether they had vampire genetics or not. He couldn't stand any other male pawing her, full fucking stop.

"Are you sure?"

He stared at his mate's practically pleading face on his mobile phone screen, not quite believing what he'd heard. "Does she know you're doing this?"

"Not exactly. She has repeatedly said how much she's enjoyed her stay, and it would be great for business having a reliable vampire community rep in Australia. She already has several contacts and could make more.

"Unfortunately, given my input in the business, we can't sponsor her. So in order to get her visa approved ASAP, she needs to get married. Then, if the guy doesn't work out, she can find a more appropriate, longer-term husband."

So, anyone half-decent would do for the interim as long as they helped her get permanent residency, but for a serious relationship, did the guy need to have vampire genetics? Did her brother's assessment of what sort of man constituted marriage material reflect her thoughts and beliefs, too?

Would she not consider a full-human guy, if she found him attractive and they connected mentally and emotionally, as well as on a practical level? Would the cultural differences be too much of a deterrent?

"Even though you don't currently know anyone, now that you're aware of the situation and the broad-reaching positive ramifications for all of us, I'd really appreciate it if you'd keep your eyes peeled for possibilities."

This guy was un-fucking-believable. Yeah, he may have a point about it benefiting their business, but he was playing his sister like a pawn. Fuck that. No way could he betray her, put her in a compromising position, unless she understood the full terms and consented.

Hang on... Why get so worked up? It didn't matter who she chose as a long-term partner. Maybe he could help her in the short term. The perfect guy, and all his positive attributes, appeared in his brain.

Someone who didn't want forever but would treat her right. Fill her in on any important details, provide respect, and factor in her opinions, keep her abreast of decisions. Make the whole experience fucking unforgettable. Make it mutually satisfying.

"Sure." Maybe the universe had heard his pleas...

Chapter Two

Temperance made a beeline for the ladies' room and shut herself in a stall, breathing hard. That man. No human male had ever had such a body-altering impact.

No Jade or Violet clan guy had either. Her brother had tried to set her up on blind dates with purely vampire heritage guys in Norway, and she'd had enough, requesting a move to work in the Australian office of his organization — out from under his well-meaning but over-controlling thumb.

She'd needed to get away, move to a place where she could start making her own decisions, free from the watchful, judging eyes of her rigid, fearful, overly traditional family.

Thankfully, Bror hadn't refused her, knowing many others with a vampire lineage lived in Melbourne, Victoria. And he saw the potential business benefits of having a hybrid rep in Australia to cater to both communities.

In terms of marrying business and personal potential, he'd hoped she'd meet someone 'suitable', which basically equated to a Jade or Violet pedigreed guy. And she wasn't against it. However, she didn't want to limit her options.

Her Jade, Violet and hybrid boyfriends had been pleasant enough but left her wanting, the sex underwhelming. She required more in order to commit to anyone—more physical, mental and emotional compatibility.

Bror could wish for whatever he wanted, but she refused to constrict her choices, refused to choose some guy who ticked all the practical boxes but didn't deliver in the desire department. Much to her family's dismay, she desperately wanted to marry for love, not status or culture or to fit in with their restrictive ideals.

Archer popped into her head—her long-standing secret crush. Not that he'd meet the commitment criteria. From what she'd seen, he epitomized 'player', with no intention to settle down. Not soon, not in the medium term, probably not ever.

She'd known her boss for almost two years and had never seen him with the same woman twice, though she doubted he'd disappoint in the bedroom. His potent virility oozed from every inch of him. And, as for her, he hardly seemed to notice her existence.

Oh, he acknowledged her, but probably more to keep the peace with, and out of respect for her brother. It made sense not to provoke your business partner.

However, the moment she'd met Archer in person, he'd imprinted on her heart. *Stupid, stupid, stupid.* Temperance hadn't even taken the soulmate serum, something that worked on everyone…supposedly. She could have, but chose fate over science, feelings over rational thinking. Always the romantic dreamer.

She still believed that a person's heart was the best determinant of love. And yet, it could be one-sided. She felt something, but did Archer? Could he? Whether he did or didn't, she couldn't turn off the Archer-admiration switch.

An element of his essence, like a weird sort of survival instinct, drew her to him like a bee to a bright, succulent flower.

How disappointing that her visa was soon to expire, forcing her return to Norway—and without even a whiff of love, without even a taste of the man she'd pined over for months.

If he hadn't been her boss and her brother's friend and business partner, she might have made her interest more obvious. But given the circumstances and her family's bias toward her finding a vampire-background boyfriend, she'd stayed silent.

Almost from the moment she'd met him, erotic dreams had plagued her sleep. She didn't literally want to sink her teeth into him, but she'd love to find out if his flavor matched his sexy cedar and sage scent.

Footsteps got louder and louder and she held her breath.

No one entered.

The footfalls passed the female staff toilets and faded into the distance. Probably one of the guys heading to the men's toilets. Was it Archer?

The man bombarded her brain in Technicolor detail, striding with self-assurance, every taut, sinewy muscle bunching and releasing, obvious even under his impeccably fitted clothes.

Everything about him exuded power, confidence, expertise. She closed her eyes and sighed. How many nights had she pleasured herself, picturing the slow glide of his hands on her body, the moist warmth of his mouth on her lips, her breasts, her pussy?

If she didn't stop that train of thought right this second, she'd have to rub her clit to climax in the restroom before returning to her desk and hope like hell no one interrupted.

Since living on her own, she fully gave in to the experience, no longer needing to muffle her moans. Each time she came, she let herself go entirely, not stifling her response.

The thought of having to keep quiet took away from hitting the ultimate height of pleasure, like attempting to restrain a sneeze. It didn't allow for the natural, uninhibited, immersive joy.

She opened her eyes and absorbed the soft lighting, the elegant and relaxed surroundings. It amazed her that more women didn't flock to the ladies' room for a bit of a time-out, a bit of peace.

While she remained alone, she debated whether maybe she *should* make the most of the opportunity? Give her flushed skin time to settle and ease the ache in her core. Otherwise, she'd squirm in her seat all afternoon, unproductive and fixated on avoiding friction, fearful she might come at the tiniest stroke of her swollen little nub.

Although highly unprofessional, it did seem like the most sensible answer, given the circumstances. As long as she focused on suppressing her vocal signs of… enjoyment.

Easier said than enacted. But the best time was now, before another staff member visited the toilet. She whipped her panties off and wound them around her wrist, then lifted her foot onto the toilet seat lid, and fingered her well-lubricated flesh.

One, two, three swipes of her clit and she came on a strangled cry, her breath sucking in and bursting out in a loud, rhythmic cycle.

"Temperance? Are you okay?" Archer's personal assistant's voice echoed in the small, enclosed space.

Oh no. "Yes!" Hopefully her breathy squeak didn't give her away. How had she not heard her approach, smelled her distinct human scent?

"When you're ready, Archer wants to see you in his office."

Again? What could he want? She'd left him less than a quarter of an hour ago. "Okay. I'll be there in a minute." *Or five.* Long enough to wipe the evidence of embarrassment from her face.

The moment the PA left, she slipped into her panties, hurried out of the stall, washed her hands and studied herself in the mirror. *He's going to know.* Something about his penetrating eyes suggested he didn't miss a thing, not the tiniest micro-behavior.

Hence why he'd been so successful. He showed a propensity for reading people's minds, thoughts, emotions. Were hers included? Or did her vampire genetics provide protection? Erect an inaccessible barrier around her brain?

She splashed cold water on her rosy cheeks and patted them dry with a paper towel. Better — *somewhat*, compared to before. She sucked in a sobering breath, pushed her shoulders back and stood tall.

She could do this. No way could he know, if she invoked her best pleasant, aloof persona. If anything, he'd fish for a response, so she couldn't react. She needed to keep calm at all costs.

Easier said than executed.

She psyched herself up the whole walk to his office and knocked on the door. Her heart thudded in her chest, rattling against the confines of her ribcage.

Instead of calling for her to enter, he whipped the door open. And oh. My. God. did he look hot. Hotter than hot. Big, buff and imposing. Shirtsleeves rolled up, tie gone, collar unbuttoned. Tattoos peeking out on his forearms and chest. She tried not to stare. She really, really tried.

"Come on in and take a seat. I need to discuss something with you."

Like what? He'd never summoned her separately before. Archer had called in the whole team, or she'd instigated approaching him with work updates as soon as they were available.

Why hadn't he mentioned whatever this was when she'd spoken to him not long ago? Had she stuffed up? Done something wrong? Nothing about his face or tone or body language gave anything away. He didn't show any signs of anger or disappointment.

Strange. What could he possibly want to speak to her about?

Instead of sitting behind his enormous desk, he sat in the visitor chair beside her, bright streams of natural light pouring over them and highlighting his summer-tanned skin. "Your brother called."

What did that have to do with her...unless? "Is he okay?" Surely Bror would have told her if anything bad had happened, but best to check.

"He's fine." Her boss—and number one forbidden crush—focused his piercing blue eyes on hers. "He mentioned your visa is due to expire."

Bloody big mouth. Her brother never could keep a secret. She had purposefully not mentioned it to Archer because she didn't want him to have any sort of hold on her...except physical. "That's right." She reluctantly spat out the words.

"Do you want to stay?"

"I can't."

"But do you want to?"

Absolutely! "It doesn't matter."

"It does. I can help you."

"How?" Why?

"I have a proposition. Come to my place tonight for dinner, and I'll explain."

Of course, in *his* home, in *his* safe haven, in private, where he had the absolute upper hand, the most control. And although it frustrated and somewhat scared her that they'd be alone together, it also sent tingles of desire arrowing down her spine, piercing her sex. "Can't you just tell me now?"

"No. I want time to go through the details, the specifics."

What details? What specifics? What on earth did he have in mind? And how much would she have to compromise to get her desired result. How much was she willing to give up, give in, concede?

She'd worked with this man long enough to know he wouldn't suggest anything that didn't benefit him in some way. No wonder the guy had a reputation as a master negotiator, except he always came out on top. So his willingness to help her wouldn't purely stem from the goodness of his supposedly caring heart.

"Will rare wagyu steak and veggies meet your nutritional needs and entice you to come?"

"I didn't commit to coming."

"Oh, you will." A flash of mischief flared in his eyes, insinuating something else entirely. Something sexual. Like he promised to thoroughly satisfy her needs, make her climax.

Unbidden heat bloomed in her cheeks. She had to be mistaken, her infatuation with the man, skewing her perception of his tone, his meaning. "Someone's cocky."

He studied her face, lingering a bit longer on her cheeks. Oh shit, he'd noticed her blush. "Not cocky... Sure, confident." And he radiated it from every pore.

Lust and curiosity tugged at her reluctance, her insecurities, encouraging her to accept his request. But should she when alarm bells blared in her head like persistent police sirens? "I can't imagine what you could possibly offer that will sort out my situation."

"Can't you?" His grin grew wider. "Then you should come and find out. I promise I won't disappoint."

Were they having the same conversation? The electricity sparking between them suggested he'd weaved in a heap of subtext, that the subjects ran parallel—the same words but totally different connotations. Or maybe he didn't intend to just tease her with innuendo. Maybe he meant both.

She subtly squeezed her thighs together and crossed her legs.

"Come on. You've got nothing at all to lose." Except time, and possibly her respectability, and the logic to make a smart decision.

Archer tempted her like Lucifer himself, offering what she desired on so many levels, whether he realized it or not. By stepping into his lair and accepting his terms, would she also be agreeing to sell her soul? Would he hand her the key to open up her options, or the key to Pandora's box?

"So what will it be? Are you willing to take a chance? Without risk, there's no prospect of positive gain."

Damn, the guy knew how to use language, use all his devilish wiles to his advantage...to perfection. She'd had limited personal exposure to Archer, yet was already practically cheerleading the guy.

From her observations, he possessed an innate ability to read people quickly, easily, efficiently, to tap into their greatest wish and pose a hard-to-ignore solution.

Temperance met his potent, waiting gaze and sighed, curiosity getting the better of her. "Fine. I'll come and hear what you have to say." It couldn't hurt, right? She didn't have to decide on anything over dinner. She'd be free to leave whenever she wanted. Make sure she factored in enough time to make an informed choice.

"See you at seven. You've made the right decision."

Only time would tell.

Chapter Three

On the way home from work, Archer stopped at the butcher to buy some fresh wagyu steaks and the fruit shop to grab some potatoes, mushrooms and silverbeet. From what he'd learned, in addition to bloody meat, hybrids loved earthy flavors.

He debated whether to buy blood pudding for dessert, not wanting her to think he was taking the piss or dissing her mixed vampire heritage. He wasn't. He wanted to tempt her, please her, lull her onto his side.

Just get it. Have it handy.

Worst-case scenario, he'd throw it out. So he added it to the shopping basket and went to the checkout to pay. When he got home, he'd hide it in the back of the fridge, and if the circumstances felt right, he'd offer her a slice or two. All of it, if that was what she wanted.

Archer lugged the shopping bags out of his car, stepped into his keyless-entry house, and disarmed the alarm system by voice command. He continued into the kitchen, dumped the bags on the floor, and put the steaks and black pudding in the fridge. He needed her onboard if his plan had any likelihood of succeeding.

He peeled and chopped the potatoes and put them on to steam, then went and had a shower. While the hot water beat down on his body and the steam billowed up around him, he debated whether to get himself off.

The woman he'd had a countless number of fantasies about would arrive at his home in less than thirty minutes. And greeting her with a massive hard-on probably wasn't the best welcome.

Then again, that might depend on whether she also lusted after him. His gut insisted it was a foregone conclusion. Solidifying his presumption, the two times he'd spoken to her in his office today, she'd displayed the classic, I'm-attracted-to-you signs—flushed face, erratic breathing and her dilated pupils had eclipsed her incredible jade, violet-flecked eyes, turning them black as onyx.

Still, he didn't want to scare her away with his overt interest. For tonight to come off right, he had to use a tactical approach. Employ subtlety, suss her out, ease her in.

He scrubbed himself clean and rinsed off, his erection refusing to subside, making his masturbation decision clear. He took his dick in hand and groaned. Fuck, thoughts of her alone had taken him to the edge of losing his load.

How would he cope with her sitting right there in his living room, looking scrumptious, and smelling like sweetness and sin all wrapped into one irresistible package?

He tightened his grip and picked up his pumping pace, imagining sinking into her snug, moist channel. One more thrust, followed by the pad of his thumb, swiping over the head of his cock, and he came.

Over the tiles, over his hand, his grunts echoing through the en suite, his breathing loud and erratic. Archer's legs shook from the force of his Temperance-inspired orgasm, and he slapped his free hand against the closest wall to stop him from dropping onto the shower floor.

He grabbed the handheld showerhead, cleaned the tiles and his hand, and finally his deflated dick. After one more thorough rinse, he shut off the taps, dried himself and raced to get ready.

Archer threw on his favorite pair of distressed denim jeans and a black body-hugging T-shirt. May as well show off his assets. He worked fucking hard to retain his fit, muscled physique. And every little one percenter helped toward his cause.

Back in the kitchen, he finished slicing the silverbeet and mushrooms, and the doorbell rang. The thrill of anticipation shot along his spine. He washed his hands and called out, "Coming!" And wouldn't that be a fucking awesome outcome.

Calm your fucking farm, tiger.

Archer invoked his cool, tranquil, confident self and walked to the door. He eased it open and — *Wow. Fuck me.*

The setting sun glowing behind Temperance, created a golden aura around her body, making her look like an angel — a sexy-as-all-fuck angel in her flowing white skirt and sleeveless, white floral top, the purples and greens bringing out the jade and violet in her spectacular eyes.

"Welcome to *huset til Archer*." 'The house of Archer' in Norwegian. He didn't know many words, but he'd use whatever he could to his advantage. Archer smiled and waved her inside.

Temperance glanced down, a shy, tentative smile on her face and went to step past him. He grasped her hand and a bolt of desire zipped through his body. She gasped, darting her gaze to meet his. No doubt she, too, had felt the power of their connection.

"You look beautiful."

"Thank you." The pulse in her wrist pounded against his thumb.

Reluctantly, he let go of her hand and gestured for her to precede him. "Straight ahead." Because, yeah, he was a greedy, pervy bastard and wanted to enjoy her from every angle.

She did not disappoint. The woman was stunning — not unusual in the vampire community. They had an innate, natural attractiveness that drew humans in like a siren song.

He'd experienced that magnetic pull with others before, but nothing had come close to the intensity he shared with Temperance. And soon — so soon he could taste it, hopefully taste her — she'd be his...if all went to his strategic plan.

They reached the living area and he headed into the kitchen. "Sit wherever you like. Make yourself at home."

She produced a bottle of red out of her cavernous bag and plonked it on the counter. Then she sat on a dining chair at the table and watched him. And fuck did he love her eyes roving over his body.

"What would you like to drink?" He imagined she'd prefer a Bloody Mary, with real animal blood in place of tomato juice over and above the red wine, but he didn't want to assume.

"What are you having?" The polite response.

"Don't worry about me. You choose what you want." And fuck did he wish she'd say, 'you' and screw the drink. Screw him instead.

"I'll have a glass of red, please."

Archer grabbed the bottle of Shiraz she'd brought and unscrewed the lid. Fuck, he loved that twist-tops had replaced corks. He pulled out a couple of glasses and filled them almost to the top. "I'll join you." Both a fact and a positive affirmation. After tonight, he hoped to be able to join her in every way possible.

Archer carried their wines to the table, and took the chair adjacent to her, keeping his glass raised. "To a mutually satisfying outcome."

She studied him, her gaze wary, but lightly tapped her glass to his. "*Skål*." Cheers in Norwegian. One of the only other words he knew well.

They each took a sip, and he couldn't stop staring at her lush lips, the rhythmic roll of her delicate throat as she swallowed.

Temperance placed her drink on the table and refocused on his eyes. "So, what's this plan of yours?"

"Let's get to know each other a bit more first, and we'll discuss the details of my idea over dinner." Because he didn't want to prematurely do the big reveal, in case he shocked her and she decided to leave early. No, he needed time to win her over.

"Just tell me now. We're alone. There's no need to drag it out."

"Humor me."

"Why?"

"Because there's no rush. We've got the whole night, and I honestly do want to learn more about you. It'll be useful, too, for what I have in mind. The better we know each other, the more likely we'll have a successful result."

She drank some wine, a confused crease marring the flawless skin of her forehead, like she wanted to probe deeper but held back.

He peered into her enthralling eyes. "I promise it'll be worth it."

"Now I'm even more curious. How am I going to eat dinner with my mind racing through every possible scenario? Or is that part of the plan? To unsettle me, rattle me, shake me to the edge of my seat, hanging on to your every word?"

He'd inadvertently instilled fear, had worried her and needed to convince her otherwise...urgently, if he had any chance of his idea working. "Quite the opposite. I want to pique your interest and encourage you to feel comfortable with me, to trust me."

"Trust you? Hard to do when you look like you want to devour me, have me on your sexual menu." He respected her ballsy, unexpected, straight-up honesty.

If she wanted to tackle truths, he'd willingly meet her head on. "You're not far wrong. I'd love to taste you, and going by your body language, you'd like me to. There's an undeniable chemistry between us.

"However, I realize it's complicated. I'm your boss, and your brother is my business partner and friend. So we can't be impulsive, can't allow lust to drive our decision-making. Hence my suggestion to get to know each other better, develop trust, clarity...consider a strategy that could meet both our temporary requirements."

Her eyes blew out broader and rounder than saucers, and she squirmed in her seat. "What sort of strategy?"

"One that factors in our attraction. Denying and avoiding the facts only makes things harder. Someone had to address the large, lustful elephant in the room."

She blinked at him, speechless, visually shocked at his candid reply.

He'd let her stew on it, give her time to weigh up the situation, her options, how much she wanted to stay in Australia. "Right now, I need to finish cooking dinner. And while I do, I want you to tell me about yourself."

"Why don't you start?"

At least she hadn't decided to high-tail it out of his house—a positive sign that he'd held her attention more than he'd aggravated her fears. He lifted an eyebrow and tried not to smirk. "Why don't *you*?"

She huffed as though exasperated. "Fine. What do you want to know?"

"Anything you choose to tell me."

"You're not making this easy."

"That's right. I'm making it worth it."

Her mouth formed the cutest little 'O', and he wanted to lean in and kiss her. Maybe later, if he were lucky. And his history indicated he tended to be a lucky bastard. He smiled and stood, turning on the stove before he gave in to his compulsion.

Archer kept quiet, waiting for her to restart the conversation. He added some salt and butter to the mushrooms, and they sizzled…a bit like the air between him and Temperance.

Patience. That was the name of this strategic game.

He put the silverbeet on to steam and refocused on the slow-cooking mushrooms. Did she feel the growing heat between them, the shift from simmering to scorching?

"My favorite cocktail is a Bloody Mary." She offered the information like a gift, a truce. An attempt to facilitate connection and move forward. And no way would he not accept her proffered baton.

"With animal blood instead of tomato juice," he said. A highly likely assumption, given the facts. But only she could confirm or deny.

"Did my brother tell you?"

"No."

"Then, how did you know?"

"An educated guess." He turned to face her and met her wide-eyed stare. "Would you like me to make you one?"

"Oh. No..." Though her eyes said *yes.* "Thank you. I need to drive home. Um...I didn't say it as a veiled request. I just thought you might find it interesting, part of understanding me better."

"I do. I find it intriguing." He really fucking did. The information... Her... Anything about her piqued his interest.

"I'm not sure how much you know about the Jade and Violet communities, but our tolerance and enjoyment of human food varies, depending on each person's palate and their amount of vampire genetics. I guess I'm one of the lucky ones. I can easily slip between human and vampire cultures because I love food...both types."

Even after all these years of knowing her brother, his friend hadn't been quite so forthcoming, quite so generous with his insider knowledge. "Good to know. Thanks for enlightening me."

"If you've got any Jade or Violet-related questions, I'm happy to answer them." She responded quickly, eagerly, nervously. So willing to please. A totally natural sub.

"Thank you. I'll definitely take you up on that, but at the moment, I want to know more about *you.*"

"Oh. Um..." She hesitated like hardly anyone had ever asked her about herself — her wants, her goals, her desires. The information he craved.

She went silent, drawing her eyebrows in and down, creating adorable crinkles in her forehead, as though she were focusing inwardly. "I love the beach, I love to swim and I love the sun."

She glanced up at him with a glowing smile. "In the past I could only tolerate about fifteen minutes of direct sunlight. But the newly developed vampire-skin sunscreen has changed that. Now, I can enjoy almost four hours of direct exposure. It's heaven."

If she thought that was heaven, wait until he got his hands and mouth on her... *If* she let him. If she not only consented to, but also desired physically exploring this powerful pull between them.

"Consider our next date a day at the beach."

"Next date? This isn't a date. This is a private business meeting." Her expressive face showed surprise yet an undeniable, wishful eagerness.

"Can't it be both? Tell me you're not attracted to me, that you don't feel the incredible energy buzzing between us, and I'll stop. I'll keep everything strictly business. But I don't think you want that, do you?"

She stared past him to the stove, then refocused on his eyes. "You'd better check the mushrooms."

Saved by sautéing fungi. *Dammit.* He turned off the heat and checked the silverbeet. *Almost done.* Time to get started on their steaks. Not that hers would take long. His either. Like her, he preferred his rare.

"Do you need a hand?"

Her hand, her mouth... "No, everything's under control. You just relax." He'd give her a mini reprieve, allow her space to process their discussion before he pitched his proposal.

Within minutes, he brought over their meals and topped up their drinks.

"That's enough for me," she said when the wine reached the halfway mark in her glass. "I've got to drive, remember?"

Even though her vampire genetics meant she processed alcohol faster, more efficiently. It took double the amount to get tipsy, let alone drunk, which suggested she wanted to ensure she could think clearly when considering his offer, and that made absolute sense. He admired her foresight...admired so many things about her already.

Temperance sliced a piece of very rare steak, sitting in bloodied juices, and took a bite. She closed her eyes and moaned, and the sexy little sound went straight to his dick. "This is perfect."

She was perfect. Perfectly sweet, perfectly endearing and, he imagined, perfectly delicious. "I'm happy it's to your liking."

"Mmm...it really is. Thank you for making the effort to accommodate me and my needs." He'd like to accommodate some of her other non-food needs, too.

"Any time."

They finished the rest of their dinner in anticipatory silence. He cleared the dishes and stacked them in the dishwasher. "Dessert now, or would you like a break first?"

"A break, while you tell me all about this offer of yours."

As in, *no more stalling*. The time had arrived. Elvis' *It's Now or Never* blared in his brain. He took a breath, organized his thoughts and propped his forearms on the counter, his gaze meeting her 'I'm-waiting' eyes.

"Marry me."

Chapter Four

"What? I thought you said *marry me*." She must have misheard. This man struggled to date, let alone speak about commitment. With her, a woman he'd hardly shown interest in, a woman he barely knew...with anyone.

A sly smile slid across his face. He was enjoying this, getting her off guard, off kilter. Keeping the control. "I did."

Her forehead crumpled with confusion, disbelief. Sure, he'd acknowledged an attraction between them — much to her surprise, considering she hadn't admitted it on her side — but she'd thought he'd propose something along the lines of a business sponsorship, not suggest they pursue a serious relationship.

"What sort of plan is that? We don't know each other well. No one will believe it. *I* don't believe it." What had prompted Mr. Anti-commitment to even suggest something so significant? He had to have his own motive.

And if, on the off chance, she agreed, would he expect them to be physically intimate? Or would their relationship be in name only, keeping to themselves in private and promoting a fake facade in public?

Just the idea of having his hands and mouth on her, sent tingles sparking in all her erogenous zones. Why? She had to have some massive unresolved issues, some masochistic tendencies, if she got excited by an inaccessible man's attention.

"You haven't said *no*, so I take that as a positive. I can work with that."

"Work with…?" She shook her head. "This is crazy." She stared at his immaculate self, his sleek, perfect environment. So out of her league. Going by her brother's off-hand comments and her observations, Archer was unlikely to find any woman suitable for more than one night.

With that realization, she should be on her guard and back far, far away. But, she couldn't ignore his indescribable, irresistible, beyond-reason magnetism. "What's in it for you?" Because there had to be something.

She wasn't delusional enough to believe he'd do this purely to help her or her brother. Not even a good friendship or business partnership would push him to make that level of personal sacrifice.

"Hear me out." He held his palms up in a placating gesture. "The easiest way for you to get a permanent visa is to marry an Australian citizen —"

"And?" She needed to hear him spell everything out, determine if his charismatic personality overrode the facts, the truth, have access to all the information and be certain before committing to anything.

"In a work sense, having a competent staff member with a vampire heritage helps us tap into a broader market and grow the company at a faster rate. And the better the business does, the better the benefits for everyone." He pulled up a chair right beside her and held her hand, stroking his thumb over her knuckles, slowly, back and forth. "You can also help me on a personal level."

"How?" She scrutinized his exotic blue eyes, her heart rate racing.

"I recently found out that I'm eligible for a significant inheritance from my great-uncle that will set me up for life, even beyond my life. But in order to access the full amount, I need to get married before Valentine's Day next year."

"That's… That's less than three months away." And she thought having six months left on her visa was cutting it super close.

"Yeah. But I figure it's this simple. We fake date for a few weeks and tell everyone it's a whirlwind romance. People love that shit."

Shit. Right. Trust a commitment-phobic player of a man to assess it that way — to cheapen any connection and relegate it to a requirement, a means to an end, a chore. "So, it's *all* fake — the dating, the engagement, the marriage."

"Not *all*. I like you…and our attraction is real. And I'm more than willing to financially compensate you for your time."

Wow. So generous. So complimentary. She tried not to roll her eyes, let the snark sneak into her voice. "So what are you saying?"

"Our *relationship* would be a mutually beneficial arrangement." He intertwined their fingers, holding her happily hostage. "Across every aspect of our lives." He brought the back of her hand to his mouth and pressed light, enticing kisses over her skin. "In other words, if we wed, there's no reason why we can't fully enjoy our time together."

Oh. Images of them naked, with Archer kissing down her bare body, bombarded her brain. "I-I never said I'm attracted to you."

He raised his eyebrows, his gaze penetrating deep into her soul. "Well, are you?"

She didn't want to admit it, so easily acquiesce, put her heart at risk. But she couldn't lie. She swiped her tongue over her bottom lip and his eyes tracked the movement. "Yes. Okay?"

His smile morphed into a wide, sinful grin. "That wasn't so hard, was it?"

Unlike his cock. Even out of the corner of her eye, she couldn't miss the big 'hello-I'm-here' bulge in his pants. Overwhelming lust had her wanting to show her appreciation. Though, she shouldn't go with her impulses, no matter how tempting.

That line of thinking could get her into trouble and be massively destructive. She needed to mull over the best course of action—for herself, first and foremost. Balancing out her heart and her rational brain. "So, now what?"

"We test the sexual waters."

"Excuse me?" Her heart rate tripled, the thudding beats thumping at her temples.

"If we go ahead with the whirlwind-romance idea, we need to look comfortable together, into each other, believable as a committed couple in public."

And what did that mean, exactly? "What are you suggesting?"

"We make sure we have sexual synergy beyond the obvious chemistry. Without it, it'll be almost impossible to keep up the charade, to convince people we're romantically involved."

"Are you talking...now?" Nerves scuttled in her stomach, but he made a good point. One that had flowed on from what she'd already alluded to earlier — no attraction, no believability, no success.

If they didn't physically gel, she definitely couldn't pretend to enjoy his closeness, his caresses, his kisses. She wasn't that good an actress.

"It's the ideal opportunity to feel each other out — figuratively and in a hands-on manner — don't you think? We're alone with no interruptions. Better to find out as soon as possible if our experiment yields successful results."

"I...suppose." She had to admit, so far, the preliminary findings looked promising. Really, really promising.

To his credit, he didn't dive in for a kiss, didn't push the boundaries. Instead, he paused, giving her time to think, to weigh up all the potential positives and negatives. "If it does, and we decide to proceed with my plan, then afterward we can work on getting our stories straight. How things progressed from work colleagues to friends, to lovers."

Any second, they'd cross that platonic physical line. Buzzing, anticipatory tingles converged in her core.

As if reading her mind and wishes, he rubbed the pad of his thumb over the back of her hand, a jolt of potent electricity sending her heart into overdrive. "I won't bite. Unless that's what you want."

Oh God.

She crossed her legs, squeezing her thighs tighter, while trying not to look as hot for him as she felt. Over-eagerness was the opposite of an aphrodisiac. When it came to Archer, from what she'd deduced, he needed something to strive for, not some woman who'd easily give in to his charm.

He stroked his thumb over the delicate, sensitive skin on the inside of her wrist, keeping his touch soft, gentle, controlled. Never overstepping, waiting patiently for her response. Her pulse took off, thumping hard and insistent.

"Mmm, this is a good sign, an encouraging sign." He stilled his thumb over her thudding pulse point and briefly closed his eyes as though tuning right into everything she wasn't saying.

"You enjoy the way I touch you. You're already aroused. I bet your panties are soaking wet." Archer stared into her eyes as though asking her to prove him wrong.

Her heartbeat went ballistic. She couldn't deny the truth. Everything he'd said was on-the-money accurate.

The slow, rhythmic drag of his thumb restarted. That, combined with his penetrating blue gaze, had her captivated, mesmerized. Her senses heightened to everything Archer—his swoon-worthy masculine scent, the raspy timbre of his voice, the increased speed and heaviness of his breathing. What would he do next? And, more importantly, how far would she let him go?

"But I won't pressure you into anything. Not my style. Consent, not force, is sexy. So I'll be guided entirely by your responses. If you want me to go further, you'll have to get past any mental hurdles holding you back. You'll have to tell me whether you want me to stop, continue, go softer, harder, slower, faster. You'll have to tell me exactly what you'd like, exactly what you want."

A rush of throbbing heat consumed her body, her fair skin, all the way to the tips of her fingers, turning a bright blush pink. The first time ever. *What is it about this man?*

She swallowed and averted her gaze, unable to continue looking him in the eye, worried she might combust. "If I agree to proceed with this expanded 'physical testing', what do you expect in return?"

"Nothing." Clear, firm, adamant...assuring. "Just your promise of passion. Consider tonight an interaction experiment. You do whatever you're comfortable with in the moment. I don't have any specific stipulations." He trailed a finger along her jaw and tipped her chin up until their eyes reconnected. "I promise I won't push you for anything—not a kiss, not a blow job, not to have sex. They'll only happen if we both want them to. Everything we do will be within your boundaries, with *your* consent."

Archer drew the softest line down the column of her throat and stopped on her breastbone. "Right now, I'm eager to touch you some more and explore. Give you the best orgasm of your life."

She attempted to keep her expression neutral but couldn't stop her toes curling in her shoes. "You're so cocky." Could she sound more breathless, more turned on?

"Not cocky, confident with my skills. I'm passionate about showing a woman a fantastic, unforgettable time, so I won't do a half-assed job. You can count on me to deliver what you've only dreamed about, to make all your wildest fantasies a reality."

A half-frustrated, half-excited moan escaped her lips. What he offered was exactly what she wished for. With his hand so close to her breasts and the rise and fall of her chest, would his fingers slip down, down, ever closer to her cleavage and dip inside her top?

Her breath faltered, and her nipples hardened into tight little peaks, chafing against her lacy bra, desperate for Archer's hands-on attention.

The man might have a shit-ton of tickets on himself, but he'd made her curious to see if he could live up to what he promised. "And what's the deal after tonight?"

"If the results are...pleasing, and we both agree to proceed with my fake-dating, marriage-of-convenience proposal, then our relationship needs to be reciprocal."

As in, full physical marital privileges back on the very accessible table, and most likely undertaken in various rooms of the house. The thrill of knowing that if she answered *yes* to his proposition, those three simple letters would act as a key, unlocking forbidden pleasure, had her heart hammering impossibly harder.

Reviewing the situation objectively, his reply was more than fair. If she went ahead with this 'experiment' and they were sexually compatible, how could she say *no* to his broader plan?

She'd commit, no question—not because she felt obligated but because she had to know whether the reality of their coming together matched the intensity of the lead up, the teasing, almost tantric-style foreplay.

Agreeing also meant guaranteed fun with Archer, for at least a few months, while possibly solidifying their serious-relationship status and increasing her chances of staying in Australia.

And if the lust fizzled and all went to crap, they had a get-out-of-the-marriage-free card. In her experience with other men, things always descended downhill once they'd passed the honeymoon period. Would Archer be any different? "What are my experiment options?"

A slow-burn smile stretched across his stubbly face. He looked at Temperance as though he wanted to strip her down and lick every inch of her skin—drive her crazy until she pleaded for more, begged him to send her over the orgasmic edge.

He leaned in, his lips within easy kissing distance. "Whatever you want."

Really? He'd let her choose *anything*? None of her previous partners had given her a sexual blank check, so much freedom of choice, had so openly and eagerly prioritized her needs.

Maybe he had honestly meant what he'd said, not that she doubted him. Everything he'd stated sounded sincere. Everything he'd done had backed his words. So far he'd given her no false promises. "To make the most of things." How would he take that?

"Good. We're on the same preferred page." He glanced between her eyes and her lips but didn't make a move, as though waiting for her to give him the 'go-for-it' green light. Behaving exactly as he'd asserted… with the ultimate restraint and respect.

His control and consideration had her craving him even more, had her developing an almost compulsion, a desire to reward him. Dangerous. The man was so incredibly dangerous. And hard to resist. "Kiss me."

Before she could take her next breath, his mouth met hers. She sighed, and he slid his tongue between her lips, his warm, sage-and-cedar scent wafting up around them, drugging her senses. He was the most delectable dish she'd ever tasted.

Archer took over, holding her face with his hands, the kiss quickly turning from slow and sweet to intense and demanding. And she liked it too much.

She whimpered, her aching, beaded nipples begging for attention. As though reading her thoughts, he traveled his hand over her top and caressed her breast. She gasped at the super-heightened sensitivity, even through fabric, and he stilled his hand.

"Okay?"

She loved that he checked, that he didn't assume. "Yes." In all honesty, she wanted his palm to slip beneath her bra.

Time to be bold, to direct what happened before the events directed her.

She grabbed his hand and guided it onto her bare breast.

He groaned. "Mmm...thank you." He zeroed in on her nipple with his thumb and finger and tugged.

She sigh-moaned and pressed into his palm.

"Fucking beautiful." He tweaked and pinched and soothed, turning her to putty in his expert hands. "Can I touch between your legs?"

She hesitated. How could she deny him? How could she deny her desires? If she did, she'd be slicing off her nose to spite her flushed face. "Yes."

He pulled back just enough to look her straight in the eye. "If you need me to stop, you tell me, and I will. I promise."

"I believe you." No one, not even the best actor, could fake the sincerity in his eyes, his voice, his actions.

"Good. Now where were we?" A devilish smile spread onto his lips right before he devoured her again. Keeping his hand on her breast, he stroked and rolled and tugged her nipple with his wicked fingers until she almost came.

Archer stopped his magnificent ministrations, and she groaned with frustration, still teetering right on the brink of climax. His raspy, arousal-infused chuckle slid over her lips, and he moved to kiss that special spot right where her jaw met her ear.

She angled her head back and to the side, giving him full access to her neck, and whimpered at the hot, wet flick of his tongue. He recommenced his hand's journey down her body and paused on her stomach.

"Lift your skirt." His urgent whispered command pelted against her skin.

She gathered up the flowy material, and he seized her mound, the heel of his palm brushing her clit, his fingers curling over her core.

"So slick. So swollen. So fucking sexy." He rubbed her clit slowly, softly, but she needed faster, firmer.

"More."

"More what?" He nipped her earlobe, a lightning bolt of desire striking deep in her pelvis.

"Pressure, speed."

"I have a better idea." He trailed a path with his lips toward her pussy and kneeled between her legs.

"What are you...?"

The glimmer in his eyes spelled out his intent without words. He wanted to taste her other lips. She probably should stop him, keep the exploration more contained and build up to something so revealing, so intimate, but her body begged her to let him proceed.

He hooked his fingers into her frilly briefs. "Lift your gorgeous ass."

She did, without hesitation, too far gone with pleasure to call off his sexual onslaught until she came.

He slid off her panties and tucked them into the front pocket of his jeans. "Spread your legs so I can look at your pussy."

No man had ever spoken to her in such a bold, direct, arousing manner. And she liked it. His words added to the intense intimacy of the moment...the excitement.

Temperance widened her thighs, fully exposing her feminine folds. Instead of diving in, he took his fill, stroking his fingers over her bare mound and teasing her soaked, engorged clit. "Mmm...beautiful."

He stared and stared, as though transfixed, spellbound by her pussy. Surprisingly, it didn't make her nervous or self-conscious. "Fuck, you smell so... Fuck...edible. I need to know if your flavor is as delicious as your scent." Before she could say anything, he dragged her butt to the edge of the seat and swooped in, burying his face between her legs.

She let out a loud gasp-moan and gripped his head.

"Oh yeah, definitely as good." He lapped at her clit, licked through to her perineum then drove his tongue inside her slit.

"Archer!"

"Mmm...you like?"

She whimpered. More like, loved. Her previous lovers hadn't come close.

He tongue-fucked her opening and swept his thumb over her clit. She detonated, riding his face and crying out in ecstasy.

Archer slipped his tongue from her entrance and groaned. "Just as I thought—fucking scrumptious. Off-the-fucking-charts. So fucking sexy."

Temperance slumped against the chair, still holding his head with one hand and her skirt with the other, breathing hard. She expected him to move away, get up, say something, but no. While orgasm aftershocks still consumed her body, he licked her clit, then took it between his lips and sucked.

Oh God. His tongue, his hot, moist mouth. Articulate in every sense. Thoroughly pleasure-giving.

She writhed against his face, a second climax surging through her body.

Archer lapped at her pussy right to the end of her release, then made eye contact and swiped his tongue over his glistening lips, slowly, provocatively. "I can't wait to slide my dick deep in here." He stroked over her entrance, and she moaned, eager to invite him to do it right now.

Except she knew him all too well. Archer loved a challenge, and the sooner she fully gave in to him, the sooner his attention would wane—the sooner he'd get diverted and move on to the next exciting new encounter. The next shiny new thing…person.

Temperance gave herself a mini pep talk, reinforcing the importance of refraining from sex, at least until they were officially married. Sure, it was fake, and a means to a mutual end, but if they were going to proceed with this charade, she didn't want to share him with other women while they were 'together'.

Not only did it look bad and diminish the strength of their 'we're-soulmates, totally-enamored-with-each-other' argument but also increased the risk of STIs.

She dropped her skirt and fixed a defiant, determined gaze on him, still kneeling between her legs, a cocky grin on his face. She didn't want his money, but she needed his guarantee of monogamy. "You've outlined your terms, and I have mine. I'll consent to your proposal if you promise to be exclusive for the duration of our arrangement and agree to no sex until our wedding night."

He stared up at her, one eyebrow cocked. The proverbial ball had bounced right back into his court. But instead of answering, he sat on his heels and waited.

A swarm of nerves converged on her solar plexus. "So, what's your decision? Is it a deal?"

Chapter Five

Clever woman. Temperance knew him better than he'd realized. She came across as sweet, innocent and a little naive, but she had gumption, smarts, spunk — an unexpected combination that turned him on even more, earning her another tick of approval beside her beautiful name.

Archer repositioned her bunched-up skirt over her thighs and stared into her eyes. "Deal."

"Really?" She looked wary, surprised, shocked.

Interesting. Had she expected him to balk at her counter terms? Try to argue and get his own way? Oh no. She'd gotten him right the first time. Nothing got him going more than an intelligent, self-assured woman with broad-minded, independent thought.

Someone who'd pose a decent challenge — or, in this case, a sexy-as-fuck challenge. A woman with insight and awareness who tasted like she did — a fucking dream.

"Yeah. It's only fair we have our own provisos that we each respect. We're setting up a two-person, equal-standing, reciprocal agreement. Otherwise, this won't work."

The sweet taste of her lingered on his lips. He already craved her again, struggled to behave, to adhere to their newly agreed terms. "Plus, our sexual synergy more than satisfied my base requirements, so I'm one hundred percent in."

She flushed the prettiest pink, bordering on fuchsia, making his dick extra swollen, extra rigid. Did she get his sexual innuendo, how much her revealing response had him practically begging for her hands-on attention?

He'd meshed with a mix of those from the Jade and Violet vampire communities, even hybrids like her, and had never seen such a telltale human sign.

Ultimately, it reinforced that she wanted him as much as he wanted her, further buoying his already inflated confidence. "Though, like I said, I won't force you to do anything. That doesn't mean I won't make suggestions. I will, but you have the final say.

"Whatever we choose to do will be a joint decision. We both need to agree." He stayed on his knees at her feet and held her hand. "I want you to feel equally involved, equally interested and open to trying things out.

"But I get you need to feel safe first. You need to trust me. And my aim is to develop that trust, make you feel secure and comfortable and cherished." Within the parameters of their agreement.

He kissed the back of her hand, returned to his chair and shifted in close. "Don't get me wrong. When it comes to sex, I enjoy taking charge, being in control, dominating my partner...but with consent. No bullying, no assuming, no abuse. No forcing. It goes against who I am as a person. I get off on giving a woman pleasure, making her feel appreciated, respected, sexy."

She smiled, her straight white teeth biting into her bottom lip, and she broke into her hot pink glow. "Thank you for being straightforward and reassuring. You've put my mind at ease."

The multiple orgasms probably helped, too. "Good." He squeezed her hand.

Her pensive violet-flecked jade eyes peered into his. "And just so you know, I do feel safe, and I trust that you won't take advantage of me. If I questioned either of those things, I wouldn't have stayed. I wouldn't have agreed to this ruse. Like you said, in order to pull this off, we need to look believable as a romantic couple, and we can't if we don't have faith in one another and feel comfortable together."

"Precisely." He pressed a kiss to her lips. "Let's move to the couch and get started on the origin-of-our-relationship story. Determine some crucial facts about each other, stuff that partners should know if they've been out on a few dates."

"Yes."

"Coffee, tea, dessert, while we work? I have black pudding."

"You do not." She stared at him with a combination of hope and disbelief.

He slapped his hand to his heart. "I do."

"It's my favorite. Did my brother tell you?"

"No. Another educated guess." Looked like pulling together key information about each other wouldn't take too long at all. Their intuition already had a head start, an accurate understanding of their individual likes and dislikes. Factoring in their cultural backgrounds.

"I can't believe you've gotten two obscure things right."

Not as huge a stretch as she believed. What person with vampire genetics wouldn't prefer a food that featured blood? "I put two and…well, as much as I could together. It's a bit like how others prefer a cheese platter after a meal instead of a dessert."

"That's it exactly. You don't necessarily know whether someone has a preference for sweet or savory, but you have parameters, indicators. And you can provide both as an option if you want. Except, in my case, I have an added genetic influence."

The taste for blood. No, not just a taste, a nutritional need. A drive to ingest red blood cells, but the quality and quantity varied. Was he worried about her feeling hungry and snacking on him?

Before he'd met several vampires and had a better comprehension of their culture, his answer would have been a resounding *yes*. But now? No.

No matter what his full-human counterparts thought, most of the Jade and Violet communities had discipline and control. They had other nutritional options. Rick Hartman, a well-known hybrid and his human business partner, Simon, had developed a range of life-changing choices.

Some staunch cultural supporters in the mortal and vampire communities refused to accept change, refused to accept different true-tried-and-tested alternatives, and he understood it, to a degree. But at the same time, it didn't support either progress or acceptance.

Archer had spoken about the need for trust, if this scheme had any chance of success, and reinforced that he had absolute faith in her. And, hand on heart, he did. Not once had she shown any disconcerting signs.

He knew of several people who'd been killed for food or changed to immortal status for a range of reasons. Mostly because the vampire wanted a companion, or a lasting love interest, or sometimes, they'd bitten a human just for fun...to see what happened. Temperance didn't fall into any of those concerning categories.

Still holding her hand, he stood and led her to the couch. "You get comfortable, and I'll get dessert ready."

Archer typed the password into his laptop, opened up a Google doc and handed the computer to her. "Start making a list of your likes and dislikes, hobbies, favorite places, what and who you find attractive, what you enjoy sexually and anything else you think is important for me to know. When I come back, we'll review your list, and I'll compile mine. Then we'll discuss what we've written, and have a live, accessible working file — something we can add to and amend as needed, something we can both refer to and memorize."

Temperance stared at the blank page, her cheeks transforming from fuchsia to neon pink — the exact shade they'd turned when he'd first kneeled between her legs. All those delightful, arousing images came flooding back, making his dick extra hard again. Time to move away before he gave in to his primal urges and pounced on her.

While he worked in the kitchen, heating slices of the pudding and making himself a coffee, she was tapping away at the keyboard. He couldn't wait to see what she'd typed — partly to determine how in tune his gut was and partly to get to know her better, particularly her preferences in the bedroom, not only to increase their chances of achieving the outcomes they desired but also to enhance every moment of their close physical time with one another.

Archer returned to her, placed his cup on a coaster on the coffee table and swapped his laptop for her plate of steaming hot pudding. He sat beside Temperance, the computer now balanced on his lap, and began reading through her answers.

Favorite place, drink, and foods, he already knew. Given she loved the beach, it didn't surprise him that swimming was her preferred form of exercise — that and bushwalking. She loved animals and hoped to get a cat if her visa was approved. And listening to music rated high on her list of likes, especially songs from the nineties.

No issues so far. He had a soft spot for animals, enjoyed a range of music, particularly nineties tracks, and liked the same activities. But he'd add one more to his favorites — sex.

Her hobbies included reading, learning new languages, discovering new places, painting portraits and volunteering at the local community center teaching about vampire culture. That's as far as she'd gotten.

All wonderful, a testament to her beautiful soul, but he needed to know more, his mind ravenous for further intimate information.

Archer glanced up and met her waiting gaze. She'd already polished off her pudding, the practically licked-clean plate on the coffee table. "How was it?"

"Yummy. Thank you. It hit the perfect spot." Exactly what he hoped to do, each and every time they got it on.

Speaking of getting it on… "You didn't mention what traits you find attractive or anything about your preferences when it comes to sex."

"I ran out of time." That glowing familiar blush — what he now referred to as embarrassed-arousal pink — invaded her face. It looked like it might stain her cheeks permanently — when around him, anyway — which he fucking liked a bit too much.

If she thought she'd gotten out of discussing her sexual likes and dislikes, she'd be in for a shock. He refused to let this subject go until he clearly understood how to thoroughly satisfy her desires.

"Don't worry. We've got all evening. Start talking, and I'll type out your responses."

"No, it's fine. Let's compile your list, and I'll add my answers onto the shared doc tomorrow."

Good try…but no. In fact, her avoiding the subject had worked out even better. Now he had the pleasure of hearing her explain what she wanted in explicit detail. So superior to reading her censored written words.

"How about we talk now, while we have the opportunity? We need to know each other inside out and back to front before we start promoting our relationship. And we need to be able to openly express ourselves, speak in detail about our proclivities, in order to make our sexual interactions as satisfying as possible…for both of us."

She let out a resigned-sounding sigh. "All right." She kicked off her shoes, curled her legs up on the couch, angled herself toward him and propped her arm on top of the backrest. "I'm going to start with traits I find attractive. I need to ease my way in."

He looked forward to easing his way in to her, too. "The floor's entirely yours." He hovered his fingers over the keyboard. Ready... Waiting...

She roamed her gaze over him and resettled on his eyes. "Physically, I prefer tall, fit guys with dark hair and blue eyes, a bit of chest hair and a sexy smile."

So...him, essentially. *Great start.*

"I like men who are confident and successful — and I don't just mean with money. I mean successful at life. Someone who isn't afraid to follow their dreams, their passion, and will persist until they reach their goal, then build...and keep building.

"Someone who will work other jobs if they need to in order to pursue their purpose. A man who's a lifetime learner and not too scared or arrogant to admit when he's wrong. A guy who strives to grow and constantly better himself and prioritizes a healthy, happy relationship with his partner."

He met all that criteria, bar one. He didn't do relationships...normally. But if he did, he'd definitely strive for a healthy, happy partnership. "Anything else?"

"He has to love animals and be supportive, trustworthy and respectful."

Archer stopped typing and grinned at her. "Sounds like me, except you missed one thing."

She rolled her eyes. "Oh, really? What's that?"

"Must be a sex god."

She shook her head, and unsuccessfully tried to hold back a smile. "Did I mention modesty and humility are essential?"

"I think I've heard of those concepts." He chuckled, and she joined in, her melodic laugh hitting the perfect notes to harmonize with his. They were literally in tune.

"Okay, I admit I might have a bit of work to do in that area, but I'm sure you'll keep me in line."

"Oh, I will. That's a guarantee."

He typed a new heading and refocused his attention on the smart, tempting, witty woman beside him, ready to resume his interrogation. What she'd hoped to avoid, he'd been hanging out to hear. "All right, talk to me about sex."

Her fingers fiddled with the fabric of her skirt. "You start."

Nope. If he explained his likes and dislikes, she could agree without offering up much, if anything, of her inner self. He refused to let her stay in the confines of her safety net. "Let's finish you first. Then we'll move on to me."

"Looks like I have no choice." She sighed with resignation and shifted in her seat.

"You always have a choice. Choose to offer up what you like…or don't. But it'll make it so much easier if you do."

Her gaze flicked to his and held. "What's most important to me is passion and an emotional connection. I want a lover who's giving, not selfish. Both parties have to want to please each other and enjoy every single second."

"And the act itself? What do you like, dislike…favorite position?"

She glanced down at her fidgety hands, a nervous laugh stumbling from her lips. "One minute I agree to dinner and a chat, and the next you're going down on me and we're speaking intimately about…everything. I didn't expect this when I agreed to come. It's confronting, overwhelming. I wasn't prepared."

He placed a reassuring palm on her knee and looked her in the eye. "I know. I sprang it on you. I realize it's a lot to digest, but you're doing great."

Her semi-shy smile was so damn cute. She stared at his hand on her leg and let out a staggered breath. "Oral clit stimulation gives me the best orgasms, the greatest pleasure. But I also love kissing, and hand and mouth attention on my breasts, my neck, my inner thighs."

Everything he'd just done, guided by his gut and years of experience. And now she'd set him the challenge of seeing whether he could add some variety to her best-orgasms list.

Her gaze flitted to his then refocused on his hand. "And I enjoy sucking cock."

Thank fuck, because he needed a woman who desired his dick in every available hole — anal included — but he got that wasn't for everyone. Didn't mean he wouldn't suss out her interest.

"When it comes to sex, I prefer face-to-face positions, especially face-to-face spooning, because looking into each other's eyes adds to the intimacy and intensity." His woman was a true romantic — the one place they didn't intersect.

"How about self-pleasure?"

Her blush intensified. "I like it. When there's no guy in the picture, I do it at least three times a week. When there is, I prefer real, warm-blooded contact, real cock. Though, my vibrator with clit stimulation is pretty hard to beat."

He chuckled. "Nice. I want to see you masturbate."

"Now?" She searched his eyes, stress radiating from her every cell.

He'd fucking love it, but he wouldn't prematurely pressure her, not until he'd determined what she could take. And always, always with consent. "Anytime. Whenever you want. I love watching a woman come."

"What if I want to watch you?"

"Just ask. I'm more than happy to oblige. Who doesn't love an orgasm? I'll take it any way I can." He stroked over his clothes-covered erection, and her eyes followed. "You watching will add to the experience."

He kept going, rubbing in a slow torturous rhythm, her gaze never leaving his little self-pleasure show. "Have you used your toys with a partner?"

Chapter Six

Her gaze jolted to his. "Um...no."

Archer stopped caressing his cock before he came and focused his full attention on Temperance. "I aim to change that. I want to incorporate your toys into our sex life. Add another dimension to the pleasure, to our connection. You happy with that?"

"I'm happy to give it a go."

"Excellent. Anything else you'd like to try?"

She hesitated and stared at her restless hands. "I've never spoken to anyone about this...um..." Temperance squirmed, the pink in her cheeks intensifying. "A blindfold, the sixty-nine position and um...anal play, if you're cool with that. If you're not—"

His fucking dream woman...if he had the inclination to stick to only one. "I'm totally cool with everything. I can't wait to share as many sexual experiences as possible with you."

She swung her gaze up to meet his, her eyes filled with visible relief, the violet flecks sparkling with undeniable elation. "Thank goodness. I worried I might freak you out."

"You'd have to do a hell of a lot more than that to scare me away." Like say the 'L' word. And he wasn't referring to 'lust'. Lust, he loved, but 'love'…scared the fuck out of him.

The commitment, the responsibility, the heightened possibility of fatherhood… Fear exploded through his body like stepping on a triggered bomb.

"Great segue into your turn." A pleased-with-herself smile stretched across her face.

Fine. He'd give her some leeway for now. He had several months to grill her and extract further personal details. The more he knew about her, the more she intrigued and bewitched him. "Bravo. Well played. I do appreciate a clever woman."

So far she'd ticked most of his girlfriend-material boxes, more than anyone he'd dated. Not that he wanted a girlfriend, but current circumstances called for one and more. "How's your typing?"

"Pardon?"

"I thought you could take over while I talk."

"Oh. Sure." She accepted the computer from him and settled it onto her lap, her fingers poised over the keys. "I'm actually pretty good." She sure was, in almost every sense.

"We actually have a lot in common. The beach, swimming, bush walking, traveling, music, pets, learning new things, helping the community. I run a business-studies class and offer free short-term mentorships to help students who are serious and ready to get started."

She stopped tapping at the keyboard and glanced at him. "That's awesome."

"It is. You get all that?"

"Sure did. I told you I was good."

"You really are." He raked his gaze over her, and she shivered. *Nice.* "Now, attractive traits. Let's see..." He drummed his fingers against his lips, his eyes taking another slow tour of her beautiful body.

"Green eyes with violet flecks, fair skin and long, bronze-colored hair. Enchanting smile, sweet personality with a dirty mind and naughty sense of humor. Sassy, intelligent, and loves sexually interacting with her partner. For me, lack of passion, lack of sexual compatibility is a deal breaker. I focus on making the most of opportunities and having fun.

"Life's too short to be serious all the time. I like a woman who's open-minded, a good communicator, passionate, driven, knows what she wants or is willing to explore options...is trusting, respectful and sincere."

She stopped typing but didn't even attempt a glimpse at him. Had she not agreed with something he'd said? Or was she nervous about what came next? What he'd reveal about his sexual appetite and tastes? And what that might mean for her.

"Ready?"

She kept her gaze glued to the screen. "As I'll ever be."

He chuckled. "Mmm...sex. I could speak about this subject forever. I find it fascinating. The many and varied pleasurable options, what people like and don't like and why, people's thoughts, beliefs and behavior. But that's a more in-depth discussion for another day. Tonight it's about you and me."

Her cheeks turned that telltale pink...again. Oh, she might have been anxious, but also interested, aroused. And he'd utilize that, funnel her wants, her needs, her desires into his future planning. *Their* future planning. Do whatever it took to get a fucking awesome outcome.

"I like intense erotic kissing, my nipples licked and sucked, love bites on my neck and chest, full-body-contact naked hugs, anal play and, last but never least, having my cock sucked. Attention to my balls while sucking me off would make it fucking perfect. Can't wait to feel your mouth on me."

She swallowed, her chest rising and falling in quick succession. His words turned her on. He bet he'd conjured up a vivid blow-job image in her mind — her on her knees, looking up at him with his dick buried deep between her lips, his hands threaded in her silky long hair, guiding her head as he fucked her sweet mouth.

He adjusted himself to relieve the pressure on his swelling cock. "And as I mentioned earlier, I love sex and eating pussy. I love getting a woman off. Gets me so hard and horny." Just talking about it now with her so close had him on the brink of coming.

"Position-wise, like you, I prefer eye contact. I agree it adds to the intensity and connection. And I want to know it's me who's giving a woman the ultimate pleasure and not some fantasy man in her head."

Her gaze met his eyes and locked. "Exactly. Whoever I'm with needs to be in the moment with me."

Excellent. They were on the same sexual wavelength. "Doggy style in front of a mirror is pretty hot — and a way of retaining eye contact in a traditionally no-eye-contact position. Plus, I find I can go deeper, which feels fucking amazing, and the change in angle hits a number of ecstasy-inducing spots for the woman. Have you tried it?"

She refocused on the computer screen, her fingers hovering over the keys, frozen. "No."

"We must rectify that, then. I'm curious to get your feedback, see if it comes close to your oral-stim orgasms. Note it down on our list of things to try together." As if he'd forget to give sixty-nine a go and do her doggy style in front of a mirror.

She cleared her throat and resumed tapping away at the keyboard. "Should we talk about our romantic-relationship origin story? How we went from work colleagues to lovers?"

A diversion. She'd reached the edge of her comfort zone, so he wouldn't push. But he would revisit. They needed to keep their conversation as flowing and uninhibited as possible if they aimed to be believable. And in order to do that, he had to make sure he set up an all-round safe environment. "Do you have any ideas? I'm open to suggestions."

Her eyes focused internally. Less than a minute later, she moved the laptop onto the coffee table and faced him, vibrating with excitement. "How about this? We were working late one night on a project with a tight deadline and, being the gentleman you are, you walked me to my car. We hadn't eaten dinner, so you suggested we grab something together and wind down. Ummm...

"I followed you to a cute little Italian restaurant and, while we chatted over a spicy meat-lovers pizza, things started to heat up. In addition to the sizzling energy between us, we discovered we had a lot in common.

"When we were done, you insisted on trailing me home and walking me to the door...for safety reasons, even though I could probably cause an attacker more harm than you ever could." Her laugh lit up her beautiful face and made her stunning eyes sparkle. He wanted to lift her onto his lap and kiss her mischievous mouth. She had him utterly enthralled.

"That awkward, what-do-we-do-now tension throbbed in the air, and we both went to speak at the same time and laughed. The laughter petered out and things got intense.

"Our gazes kept shifting between each other's eyes and lips, and we leaned in as though drawn by a strong magnetic force. We kissed, and it was magic, sealing our fate. We've been almost inseparable ever since." An eager expression filled her irresistible face. "How's that?"

"Sounds like you've been reading too many romance novels."

Her eyes went wide, and her mouth gaped open, as in, you-have-got-to-be-kidding-me — and he absolutely was.

"I'm joking. That was fucking brilliant! I think I need to promote you to Chief Communications Officer."

They both laughed, then almost exactly re-enacted the scene she'd described. Their gazes flitted between each other's eyes and lips, and they met in the middle of the couch, slamming their mouths together in an urgent, frenzied kiss.

Before they got too carried away, he broke the hot-as-fuck lip lock, and she let out a little groan of protest. He could totally relate. "Quick, you better get our version of events down before we forget the details." He held her face and stroked his thumb slowly, back and forth, over her parted lips. "Then we can get back to this."

She shot out of his arms, kneeled in front of the computer and frantically recorded the story she'd concocted. He'd never witnessed anyone's fingers fly so fast across a keyboard.

Temperance reread what she'd written to him to check if she'd missed anything or he wanted to add more, then saved. He had his docs set to auto-save but best to be on the overly safe side.

"Come here." He patted his lap in invitation. "Let's continue where we left off."

She jumped up and straddled his thighs, her skirt flowing over his legs and spilling onto the couch, her bare pussy brushing his confined cock. "How do you want me, Sir? Like this?"

Sir. Fuck. Oh, he wanted her every which way she'd allow him. "Yeah, but preferably naked."

"I don't think that's a good idea." Except her eyes, and the subtle grind of her hips against his dick said the exact opposite.

"On the contrary. I think it's a great idea." He took her lips in a scorching hot kiss, and she melted against him.

They made out — best make-out session he'd had, and he'd experienced a shit-ton — and mindful of respecting her wishes not to go too far, too fast, too soon, he summoned the strength to override his compulsion to mark her as his and slowed down the pace.

She looked all soft and floaty and drugged on lust — and so damn beautiful. Fucking irresistible.

Mine flashed into his head. Yeah, total possessive, primitive caveman, desperate to claim his territory.

She shifted on his lap, her pussy brushing his dick. One of his hands clamped tight to her face, the other to her ass, in an attempt to hold on to his fraying thread of control.

Temperance didn't seem to notice how close he'd come to caving in to lust. How close he'd come to forgetting all they'd spoken about, stripping her naked and showing her how amazing they could be together.

She looked at him with wide, eager eyes. "We should take lots of photos, too, with both our phones. Selfies, as well as pictures when we're out with friends and attending events. They'll provide additional proof."

"I like the way you think. Excellent idea." Archer wrapped one arm around her waist, holding her in place and leaned forward to snatch his phone off the coffee table.

"You're not going to take one now? I must look like a disheveled mess." She attempted to straighten her top, and finger comb her sexily mussed hair.

"I am." Using one hand he opened his camera app, switched the setting to selfie, and raised his arm, angling his mobile until it showed them on screen. "Snuggle in close."

"Wait." Temperance held up her hand, half obscuring her face right as he took the first pic.

"Did you take one already?" She stared at him in horror, and he snapped again.

"Stop it!" She laughed, and he snapped another shot.

He laughed, too, and took a few more pics.

She buried her head into his neck, her palm, pressed to his chest, and he captured a couple more candid shots.

She partially tilted her head and peered out. "Am I safe?"

"For the moment." He liked that she could muck around, and fuck, she felt good plastered to him. Their play time over the next few weeks was going to be so much fun.

"Let's review the pictures." He lowered his phone, waited for her to focus on the screen and flicked through the cool collection of photos. Surprisingly, they looked like a believable, totally-into-each-other couple.

"They're actually not too bad." Temperance sounded amazed.

"I agree. We look natural and comfortable together. They'll do the job."

"Oh. Yes." Her smile suddenly looked forced, brittle, like it might break.

He tipped her chin up and searched her eyes. "Everything okay?"

"Why wouldn't it be?"

"I don't know. You tell me."

"I guess I'm...I'm just tired. It's been a long, challenging day, filled with a number of unexpected surprises." She went to get up. "I should go."

Archer clamped his hand onto her thigh. "Haven't you forgotten something?"

Her forehead furrowed as though she'd racked her brain for the answer. "I don't think so."

"I know so." He trailed the pad of his thumb over her lips, then slowly lowered his mouth to hers.

She closed her eyes, her lips parting on a sigh, and he slid his tongue inside her mouth. He licked and teased, eliciting a guttural groan from her throat, making his dick throb. But instead of stroking his cock to completion, he slipped his hand beneath her skirt, zeroing in on her cream-covered clit.

She startled, then bucked into his palm with a whimper. He rubbed her slick, swollen flesh with his fingers, and took charge of the passionate kiss, quickly bringing her to an orgasmic crescendo.

Temperance came all over his hand while he swallowed her moans of pleasure. He would love to treat her, and himself, to this each night...and day. They hadn't specified how much time they'd spend in each other's company, but he hoped it'd be heaps. Whatever it was, he planned to maximize every single moment.

She slumped against him. "Mmm...how did I forget *that*?"

"No idea. But something tells me it won't happen again."

"Consider a thorough goodnight kiss part of our fake relationship package."

"I will, and I do."

She sighed, the sound full of deep satisfaction. "I'm so boneless right now. You might have to carry me to the car."

Wearing her out with pleasure—fucking best compliment. He peppered kisses over her temple, her hairline. "Whatever you want, baby." Clutching her close, he strode to her compact sedan and deposited her in the driver's seat, with the promise of more touching and kissing tomorrow. And he couldn't fucking wait.

Chapter Seven

The drive home was an afterglow-charged blur. Temperance made it to bed and fell into a comatose sleep. She woke, refreshed, re-energized, though a little groggy, like she'd had a huge night on *real* Bloody Mary's and still remained a little intoxicated.

And she was, but not with alcohol, not with vampire-specific stimulants—with Archer. That man had the most panty-melting voice, the most skilled hands, the most talented tongue.

A reel, reliving their interlude, had her body tingling in all the right places. And she'd see him again soon. Unfortunately, only in a workplace capacity.

But she shouldn't complain. If they weren't employed in the same organization, it could have been hours before she'd get her next Archer fix.

So greedy.

Oh. *Oh shit.* She threw her forearm over her eyes and plummeted back to earth. She'd made a massive, self-absorbed mistake. He'd had her so high on endorphins that she hadn't even thought to offer him some relief.

Yes, he'd promised her he hadn't expected anything in return, but now she wished she had reciprocated — using her own initiative, of her own volition. She wanted to treat him as much as he'd treated her, have him feel equally as elated.

Maybe his statement had a reverse-psychology effect?

No, not only that. He'd honored his promise, his actions selfless, considerate, trustworthy — traits she hadn't been sure he possessed. And because he hadn't pushed, because he'd focused purely on her pleasure, she couldn't wait to return the favor.

The anticipation of seeing Archer and how things progressed, had her flying out of bed, getting ready in a flash and making it to the office early. She parked her car in the staff parking lot and sensed someone watching her.

She shot her gaze as subtly as possible around the area but didn't notice anyone or anything out of place. Strange. She'd had the feeling before, in Norway and even since she moved to Australia, reminding her of her clingy ex, Beau.

But she hadn't seen him for years, and by all accounts he still lived overseas and had moved on, relationship-wise. So she had to be imagining things, making unfounded associations.

Alone and safe in the lift, her heart rate settled, and her mind drifted to how carried away she'd gotten with the slightest touch of Archer's hand.

If she hadn't left when she did, they'd have torn off each other's clothes and wound up in his bed...for certain. Luckily he'd shown some restraint, because she'd been moments away from giving in to her urges.

Exactly the opposite of what she'd promised herself and confidently assured him. Exactly the opposite of what she needed to do.

Given the natural attraction humans had to vampires, she'd expected Archer to succumb to the lust spell, the power like an irresistible force. But her? A stupendous surprise. In past relationships, she hadn't experienced anything near the pull, the intensity, the level of responsiveness she had with her brother's friend, her boss.

The elevator slowed to a stop, the familiar ding announcing her arrival. The doors slid open to a super quiet reception area. She walked to her office, her heels clicking on the timber floor, breaking the silence.

After logging in, she scanned through her emails. Archer had requested an impromptu, urgent staff meeting for nine a.m. *Unusual.* Worry gnawed at her stomach. Had the business suffered a setback while he'd been busy entertaining her last night? Had something catastrophic happened following her departure?

Guilt and curiosity fought for supremacy in her mind, and she had to find out the truth, preferably before the meeting. She made a beeline for Archer's office and knocked on the door.

No answer.

"Archer?"

Nothing. She knocked again, opened the door and peered into darkness. Her eyes adjusted, searching the space and finding it desolate, empty. He must have sent the meeting request from home. She returned to her desk and tried to work, while keeping an ear out for his deep, distinctive, Dom-like voice.

Staff started trickling in, but she'd seen no sign of him...yet. Five minutes before the meeting, she made a special black vampire-blend coffee and took a seat in the bustling assembly area.

Going by the chitchat, no one had any idea why he'd called them together first thing in the morning. Fear-laden rumors flew around the room, questioning the stability of the business and whether Archer would announce a need for tightening spending, staff cuts, redundancies.

The man of the moment made an entrance right on the dot of nine, and everyone went silent. His neutral facial expression gave nothing away. He strode to the front and faced the group. "Thank you all for coming at such short notice."

Archer made eye contact with a range of employees but still hadn't looked at her. Why? Had he not noticed she'd arrived, that she sat within meters of him? Or had he thought things through overnight and changed his mind?

"I have an important announcement to make." He scanned the crowd, and stopped on her, his penetrating gaze boring into her eyes. "Temperance, would you please join me?" He extended his arm and beckoned her to approach him, the hint of a smile on his gorgeous, tempting lips.

All eyes focused on her, while she sat frozen in her seat. What did he have in mind? Most likely something publicity related, given her role. Maybe he'd formally acknowledge her promotion to Chief Communications Officer. Hopefully no one saw his decision as nepotism, because he definitely hadn't offered her the position as part of their *deal*.

First and foremost, like her brother, he was a businessman and focused on putting the right people in the right roles to maximize the company's outcomes.

"Temperance, please." He waved his hand, encouraging her over.

She stood on shaky legs and made her way to him, her vision blurry on the edges, as though coated in Vaseline. When she reached the front he mouthed *thank you*, and she shot him a 'what's-going-on' glance.

"It's a surprise, baby," he whispered so only she could hear.

What was a surprise? She turned to smile at her colleagues, trying not to appear totally perplexed, trying to reassess if any of them might know something, give something, anything, away.

Whispers started up again, people speculating, guessing, intrigued, the noise in the room rising.

A couple of staff stood up at the back, their phones focused on her and Archer. Were they filming?

Archer wrapped his arm around her waist and held her tight to his side, eliciting a few *oohs* and *aahs* and *ohs* from the crowd.

"Everyone, can I have your attention, please?" His powerful voice broke through the chatter.

The room throbbed with enthralled silence.

"I want to share some happy, exciting news." He glanced at Temperance with an elated grin. "I'm thrilled to tell you that we—" He squeezed her hip. "We're a couple."

The area erupted with cheers and claps and well wishes.

"When did you start seeing each other?" someone called out.

"Recently, but our attraction has been simmering away below the surface for a while." Archer spoke smoothly, confidently addressing the jostling, small-yet-curious, audience, while she stood there mute. His announcement was a surprise, all right.

"Why tell us now, when your situation is so new?" someone else asked.

"I wanted to get it out first before any rumors started." He rubbed her back with warm, slow, soothing strokes.

The muscles in her shoulders and neck relaxed. She hadn't realized they were so tense.

"So, it's a whirlwind romance? How romantic!" Archer's secretary gushed.

Archer glanced at Temperance, his eyes filled with authentic adoration, then refocused on his personal assistant. "I know it sounds cheesy and clichéd, but yeah. Up until now I didn't believe anything like this was possible, especially not for me."

"Looks like you've finally lost your number one spot on the eternal bachelor list," the finance manager said.

"You're officially off the market. It happens to the best of us," the HR manager chimed in.

"It does indeed." He pressed a tender kiss to Temperance's forehead.

More claps and cheers filled the compact, usually stark, clinical space.

"Before we wind this up and get back to work, there is one additional announcement I'd like to make." Archer let go of her, his smile wide. "Please put your hands together and congratulate Temperance on her promotion to Chief Communications Officer."

Clapping and shouts of praise ensued, her face heating to epic-embarrassment proportions. The timing was not ideal, following his 'we're a couple' confession. With her brother and her 'boyfriend' co-owners of the business, the whole thing screamed of favoritism.

"Since Temperance arrived at our Australian office, she has consistently produced exceptionally high-quality outcomes. She deserves official recognition for her workplace achievements. I believe the business will flourish as a result of her taking on this new portfolio, and everyone else will also benefit. The better the company does, the more bonuses and promotions become available."

More whoops and cheers bounced around the room. Archer stood by her with a huge smile, clapping with sexy, honest enthusiasm.

She needed to say something, acknowledge the staff support and show gratefulness and appreciation — demonstrate that her personality and work ethic hadn't changed. If anything, they'd improved.

Anxiety gripped her stomach, clamping invisible hands around her throat, but she had to push through. "Thank you so much for your belief and trust in me. I plan to continue to prove why I'm so well suited to this public relations position, why it makes sense to retain me in this role."

"You're a natural." One of the women's voices carried across the small, hyped-up crowd.

The meeting had morphed into a team bonding session. And from her experience, if an organization had a harmonious culture, it tended to directly correlate with productivity — a great outcome for staff as well as for the business.

Archer wrapped his arm around her waist again, sending a jolt of awareness to her core. Even for that short amount of time, she'd missed his touch. Had he missed hers, too, or was he purely playing the enamored boyfriend part? "All right everyone, time to get some work done. Any questions or concerns, please come and see me or speak to HR."

Staff started filing out of the room, taking their lively chatter with them. Archer turned to her and swept a loose lock of hair off her face. "Sorry to spring that on you, but I thought, this way, your reaction would come across as more sincere. You did well, baby."

Tingles lit up her lady bits. She really, really liked how he said 'baby' with that low, raspy rumble. He'd done it a few times now, and she couldn't imagine ever getting sick of the endearment. "Thanks—"

"We'll text the clips through," someone said.

Her gaze darted to the door, the last person to exit holding up his phone on the way out. One of the two staff who had apparently filmed the whole thing.

"Thanks, mate," Archer replied and immediately refocused on Temperance. "Come to my office."

She met his probing gaze. "After what you've just broadcast, don't you think that'll look a bit suspect, unprofessional?"

"No. We work together, and we're seeing each other. It's the one spot we can speak without interruption. We're not sneaking around. We've been upfront...for the most part. If people want to imagine what we might get up to, let them. As long as we're not slacking off, as long as our work gets done, it's not a problem."

"I suppose..." She glanced at the door, double-checking they were alone. "Did you recruit those two staff members to film us?"

"Not just us, the whole situation. I figured capturing some clips in addition to snapping some pics, would build a strong evidence base."

Smart, strategic, sexy. A triple threat. And a huge worry for her ridiculously romantic heart. "I like the way your mind works." *Mostly.*

His blue eyes flared with obvious desire. "I don't think that's all you like."

Correct. So correct. His hands, his lips, his tongue... She appreciated his whole package, more than she should. She couldn't wait to test-ride his cock...once they'd tied the knot.

Not before. *Definitely* not before. She had to call on all her reserves of strength and not waver, not give in to her overwhelming attraction to Archer. Her decision-making had a significant impact on whether she had any chance of a real relationship with him long term. Although idealistic and naive, that was what she wanted — him, in her life, as her eternal, monogamous partner.

As screwed up as it sounded, even in the short time she'd really known him, she saw potential. Though, come February, her opinion of him might change. And, of course, he needed to reciprocate, which she had absolutely no control over.

"Let's finish this conversation in private. I have something else to tell you." Before she could reply, he grasped her hand, intertwined their fingers, and strode to his office. Once inside, he shut the door, took a seat in his fancy leather chair and patted his thighs.

She hesitated. "What if someone comes in?"

"They won't. They'll call or knock first." He extended his arms, beckoning her. "Come on. My lap's getting cold."

She held still, watching, deliberating — then, as requested, came and sat across his legs. He slid his palm along her outer thigh, and she shimmied in closer.

"Much better."

She agreed.

Archer crept his hand beneath her skirt and kept it on the outside of her knee. He curled his other arm around her and held her hip. She wasn't going anywhere, and she liked it. Going by her body's response, she liked being imprisoned on his powerful legs and pressed against his steel-hard abs, his pulsing, erect cock.

She wound her arm around the back of his neck, bringing their faces so close, his breath caressed her lips. "So, what did you need to tell me?"

"It's been too long since I last made you come."

Her heart raced and she squirmed, her hip nudging his extremely eager erection through his tailored pants. "Really? That's the important information you needed to impart?" Her breathy answer contradicted her 'you've got to be kidding' words.

"And I need to lick your pussy, top up on your taste."

"Be serious."

"I am. Too many hours have passed since you came on my face. I'm suffering major withdrawal symptoms. I need a fix so I can concentrate and get some pressing work done."

"So what do you expect me to do? Take off my panties, lift my skirt and bend over your desk?"

"Yeah, that'll work."

"Archer!" Her supposed shocked response totally lacked conviction.

A devilish grin tugged at the corners of his lips. "And, I applied for our marriage license."

Oh. Wow! He *was* serious. About their agreement, anyway. "You did? When? This morning? Is that why you came in a bit later than usual?"

"Yes, yes, yes. And now I want to hear *you* say it."

She rolled her eyes and shook her head, unable to wipe the smile from her face. "How long until we receive official approval?"

"We should get the go-ahead to marry in a month." He walked his fingers down her arm and grasped her hand. "So, now that we have the formalities out of the way, just say *yes* to some fun. Indulge me." He pressed her palm to the bulge in his pants. "Feel how much I want you."

So big. She'd feel every thick inch of him...when the day came.

He groaned. "Get up, give me your panties and get in position."

She forced a stern expression. "I want my undies back this time. You can't steal all of them."

"What a shame."

She squinted her eyes at him but stood and complied, sliding her panties down her legs and giving them to his grabby outstretched hand. "Mmm...so wet." He brought her bunched-up briefs to his nose and growled. "Fuck, you smell *so* good."

He pressed his palm against her lower back and gently pushed.

She folded forward, stretched across his desk, and gathered up her skirt, fully exposing her butt and pussy.

"Fucking beautiful." He rolled in close, massaged her bottom with his big, warm hands, then reached around and trailed a couple of fingers from her clit to her entrance, gathered up some of her juices and slowly dragged them between her butt cheeks. With one finger, he thoroughly coated her rear hole and continued to press and play.

A shiver of delight raced up her spine, and she gripped onto the far edge of his desk. No one had gone there before. She'd wondered about it but had never had the guts to ask a boyfriend to explore the usually taboo area.

Until him. Until he'd shown interest in what she wanted. Unsurprisingly, she liked it...a lot. The fact that it was Archer touching her forbidden spot made it even more sublime.

He turned her to face him then his hot breath caressed her clit before he took her wanton little nub in his mouth and sucked.

She let out a cry and gasped.

"Relax. No one will hear." He spread her folds and glided his tongue to her entrance, where he licked and lapped and teased.

She bucked into his face, and he speared her opening right as his finger breached her back hole. "Oh!"

"Just go with it. I promise you'll enjoy the ride," he said, and proceeded to tongue-fuck her entrance while he softly finger-fucked her ass.

The beginnings of an orgasm burgeoned in her core, but she required more clit stimulation. "Make me come. Please," she pleaded.

"What do you need, baby?"

Of course he wanted to hear her say it. Her desperation to climax pushed her past any reticence, any embarrassment about admitting what she craved. "Your tongue on my clit."

"Good girl." He licked back to her engorged flesh and flicked his tongue hard and fast, his finger still thrusting slowly and gently in her ass.

Not even ten seconds later, she shattered, grinding against his face and his finger and groaning his name.

"Mmm...my morning tea came early," he murmured and continued licking.

Her breathing slowed as she reached the end of her magnificent, all-encompassing release, and he kissed her clit.

Archer slid his finger from her still-pulsing sphincter and slapped her ass.

"Oww!" She whipped her head around. "What was that for?" she said, rubbing the stingy spot.

"To ground you before you leave my office. Otherwise, you'll float out of here on cloud fucking nine, silently announcing to everyone what we've been up to."

Oh. Fair point. Thankfully one of them could think rationally. Euphoria had a way of overriding caution and sensibility, creating a sort of risk amnesia. As the boss, he needed his total wits about him to respond to anything that arose. As an employee who'd recently been promoted, as well as girlfriend to the boss and sister to one of the company owners, so did she.

Archer, Bror and now her, to a certain extent, needed to quickly address an unexpected crisis, call an emergency meeting, make an urgent, important decision. As the leaders of the company, her brother and boyfriend needed to take on extra responsibility. But once Archer stepped outside of work, she'd give him a well-deserved break, some hands-on, mouth-on relief.

He rolled back, giving her some room, and she stood and smoothed down her skirt. She held out her hand to him. "Panties, please."

"Kiss me, and I promise I'll return them to you tonight, when I come to your place for dinner."

"Why not now? What are you planning to do with a worn, skimpy scrap of lace? Use it as smelling salts?"

"Among other things." He winked, a roguish grin growing across his gorgeous face.

All sorts of X-rated images slammed into her mind. Would he use her panties to caress his cock while he masturbated, his spurts of cum coating the flimsy material?

She could hardly stand still, her clit throbbing for renewed attention. How did he always have the upper, very skilled hand?

Temperance huffed out a breath, but internally, she loved the playfulness between them. None of the relationships with her exes had incorporated this much freedom and fun. Everything about Archer was new and exciting…except his allegiance to bachelorhood.

She stepped between his legs, held his designer-scruff-covered jaw and licked the seam of his lips before sliding her tongue between them. He gripped her hips and took over the kiss, slanting his mouth and driving his tongue deeper.

Temperance wanted to straddle him, her breasts pressed to his chest, her pussy rocking against his cock. But that would only cause trouble for both of them. If he came in his pants, he risked a potentially awkward, visible, uncomfortable wet patch, and if he didn't, she'd most likely give in to lust, rip open his fly and slide down onto his dick.

She abruptly broke the kiss and stepped out of their intimate embrace. "I need to go before we get too carried away."

"You're right. We should definitely save something for later." His raspy tone and fully dilated pupils disagreed with his words.

Knowing him, even in this short time, he'd always have something up his sexual sleeve. And didn't that fire up her libido and keep the sexual fires burning…

Chapter Eight

Archer arrived at Temperance's apartment situated in a large, impressive complex — more like a resort than a residential high-rise building — and pressed the intercom. Almost immediately she buzzed him in, and he rode the swift elevator to her floor.

No wonder she'd chosen this place, overlooking St. Kilda beach. He exited the lift and strode to her door, as though he hadn't seen her for days, not just a few hours. Until her, no woman had had him so...pussy struck.

Now that he'd touched her, knew how incredible she tasted, how well she responded to him, he couldn't get enough. It was as though her touch, her scent, her juices had addictive properties. And maybe they did. It would explain why his attraction to her had escalated so quickly and held so strong.

He reached her door and knocked. She swung it open, looking sweet yet sexy in leggings and a tank top that conformed to her every curve. Simple, yet sensual to the fucking max.

The waif look had never done it for him, and he wasn't pro Rubenesque either. According to his attraction barometer, Temperance had exactly the right proportions.

"Come in." She stood back, holding the door open, and waved him inside. Her home, *wow*, it symbolized her perfectly with its cool, yet simple, welcoming tones and pristine yet cozy vibe.

The blue, white and aqua color scheme reminded him of the beach. It had the same feel as a penthouse he'd stayed in at the Whitsundays in tropical north Queensland.

"Would you like a tour or should we order something to eat first?"

"Let's order, then you can show me around while we wait." And hopefully also fit in some hands-on play time. Since when had he ever experienced this level of withdrawal? Usually once he'd had a taste of a woman he happily moved on. Maybe his interest lingered because they hadn't had sex?

They decided on some steaks and salads provided by super-convenient, easy-as-fuck-to-access Uber Eats, which he insisted on paying for, seeing he'd invited himself over. After an initial protest, she conceded, realizing he wouldn't budge, and made them both a Bloody Mary.

Standard for him, extra bloodied for her. They toasted to their proposed upcoming nuptials and had a sip of their drinks — strong, just how he liked it — then epitomizing an expert tour guide, she took him through her two-bedroom apartment.

The decor theme continued right through the space, like a rolling wave. So unequivocally her.

She led him into her bedroom, the large window boasting spectacular beach views, and they placed their finished drinks on the closest bedside table. "If you think it's nice now, wait until dusk."

Unsurprising that twilight, transitioning into evening, was her preferred time. It'd probably been wired into her vampire DNA. Add the night lighting and...spectacular. Not as breathtaking as her but still striking. He reached out, cupped her delicate jaw and drew her to him.

If he had his way, he'd strip her naked, press the front of her body against the window and take her from behind. But, unfortunately, tonight wasn't Archer's choice. It fell in the realm of Temperance's choose-her-own-adventure.

She'd made it clear she wanted to hold off on sex until they officially married, and he'd respect her wishes. There were heaps of other fun things they could do instead. And he planned to try as many variants, permutations and combinations as possible. When it came to sex, he'd shown a natural propensity for inventiveness.

Archer dipped his head, locking his lips to hers, and what was meant to be a light, teasing kiss turned hot and heavy and intense fast. He plastered her to him, lifting her just enough to grind her clit against his cock.

And *fuck me*, the friction had his balls tightening with the urgent need for release.

No. Not fucking yet. He had to hold off. Dinner would arrive any minute, and he didn't want to rush. After they ate, they could take their time, undressing, exploring, savoring. Coming.

The intercom buzzed, as if on cue, and he halted their fucking-hot frottage session. She whimpered in protest, and he could entirely relate. They were both breathing hard, worked up, so close to climax...and deprived of the ultimate ending. Kind of like extreme edging play—frustrating in the short term, mind-blowing in the long term.

The buzzer went off again.

"Shit!" She escaped his embrace and raced out of the room.

He took his time, picked up their empty glasses and sauntered into the living area to find her hovering by the closed front door, bags of food in hand.

Archer put the glasses on the table, then wrapped his arms around her from behind and spoke softly in her ear. "We'll pick up where we left off after we eat. I promise the delay will be worth it."

Her breath caught, and she shivered.

He extricated their food from her grasp and filled their plates while she topped up their drinks. Once everything was sorted, they sat at her white, wooden table and dug into their steaks, both starving. At least, he certainly was...for fuel and for further sexual contact.

"Have you told my brother about us?" she asked in between mouthfuls.

"Not yet. I thought we should do it together."

"What are we going to tell him, exactly?" She paused, mid forkful.

"That we're seeing each other." He shoveled another delicious scoop of meat and salad into his mouth.

"Don't you think he'll be suspicious? He just asked you about helping me to stay permanently and all of a sudden we're dating?"

Possibly. Probably. But it didn't change anything. It might not be the outcome Bror preferred but, ultimately, Archer's intervention would help her remain in the country, which was supposedly what he wanted. What they all wanted.

"Let him think whatever he likes. We can't afford to explain our little secret to anyone in case it somehow gets out. And, I also don't want to put people in a position where they feel they have to hide anything about us."

"I suppose. It's just, he's my brother and we're close. I don't like lying to him."

"You're not lying. We *are* seeing each other…" Were they ever, much to his horny little internal devil, his greater satisfaction, gratification. "And we're in a relationship of sorts. Just a few additional stipulations only we know about and that's normal for couples. I'm sure you don't tell your brother all the ins and outs of your intimate relationships. Do you?"

"No. Of course not. That would enter into the realm of too much information and betray my partner's trust."

"Exactly. We all pick and choose the level of detail we give others, depending on the circumstances."

She looked him in the eye. No wavering, no hesitance. Pure decisiveness. "We should video call him tonight before he hears it from one of the staff members."

"Good idea." Not just that. They needed to try and get Bror onside as soon as possible in case they required extra support and backing for their 'relationship'.

They finished their meals, wiped down the table and loaded the dishwasher. She grabbed her phone and sent her brother a message to check if he was free to chat.

He responded 'yes' within seconds, and she sent him a video call request.

Here goes…

Bror answered, and she kept the phone trained on herself.

"Hey, Temp, what's up?"

"Can't I just call you to say *hi*?" Her voice staggered with nerves, with classic defensiveness.

"Yeah, but you rarely do. You usually have some news to tell me, need a question answered or require my opinion on an issue." He'd totally picked up that something was off. Weird. Different. The pros and cons of being close to someone.

A civil, pleasant smile slid onto her face. "Today is a news-telling day."

"Good news, I hope." Pretty much confirming Bror had seen through her all-is-fine facade.

"I hope you agree it's great news." She angled the phone to include Archer in the picture.

A crease split his friend's forehead. "Oh, hey, Archer."

"Good to see you, mate."

"So what's this news? I'm guessing it's some Australian-arm, business-related thing."

"Umm…no, actually. Archer and I —"

"We've started seeing each other." Archer finished the sentence for her, refusing to pussyfoot around the situation. Refusing to play any guessing games. Refusing to tiptoe around their agreed relationship. They needed to promote it as best they could from as early as possible.

"Romantically?"

"That's right." Archer put his arm around her and pressed a kiss to her temple.

"That's…unexpected." And obviously not approved, going by Bror's crumpled, contorted facial expression. "When did this happen?"

"Recently. Though, from my side, the attraction has simmered for a while." *Not a lie.*

"Really? From before or after I asked you to help Temperance with her visa?"

"Before, but we didn't realize both of us felt something for each other until around the time you spoke about her visa limitations." *All true.*

Bror rubbed his cleanly shaven chin. "I see." The guy appeared to cycle through possible options, but not backing them would jeopardize Temperance's ability to obtain permanent residency.

Checkmate. He could no longer avoid the circumstances, no matter how much he wanted to. Either he chose to support his sister staying or he didn't.

Temperance stared at her brother with full conviction. "We wanted to tell you before you heard it from someone else."

"I appreciate that." His smile looked forced. "Temperance, can I speak to you alone?"

Chapter Nine

"Of course." Temperance held the phone to her top and shot Archer a panicked stare.

He put a reassuring hand on her upper arm and mouthed, "You'll be fine."

She hoped so. Obviously her brother disapproved. Archer was his friend but had no vampire genetics, which apparently took him out of the running for an acceptable romantic partner.

A Jade or Violet descendant was usually a requirement in her family, but because her brother knew and liked Archer, she'd assumed he'd be more open...flexible.

How would she deal with Bror's...rigidity? Did he want to grill her in private, make sure she wasn't coerced? Question their story? Question her thinking, her choices? Try to talk her out of committing to Archer?

She entered her bedroom, shut the door and schooled her features into what she hoped looked like a relaxed, I'm-cool-with-this expression.

Temperance sat on the bed and brought her brother's face back into view.

"You're alone?" His concerned violet, jade-flecked eyes bored into hers.

"Yes."

He sighed. "Are you sure you know what you're doing?"

"Excuse me?"

"Getting involved with Archer."

"I'm not 'getting' involved. We *are* involved."

He scrubbed a hand over his face and raked his fingers through his short dark hair. "I can't say I'm happy about it."

"Why? Isn't he your friend?" *Dial down the defensiveness.* Or he'd never take her seriously, never accept her as an adult, an equal. "You care about him, and you care about me — or so you say. So I thought you would have been thrilled to hear we were together. Don't you want us to be happy?"

"Archer *is* my friend, and that's why I'm worried. He loves no-strings-attached sex. He loves women...different women. He loves his bachelor lifestyle. As long as I've known him, he's never dated someone for more than a couple of days, not even that. He'd be lucky to have gone out with a woman more than once. He's a short-term, hook-up type."

Bror stared at her with a brotherly, I-feel-for-you, you-are-so-gullible stare. "Don't get me wrong, I love him, but I especially love you, and I don't want to see you hurt."

"More like he's full human, right? Not *suitable*. Not *good enough* for me." She shook her head in disgust. "I know what I'm doing." *Mostly.*

He sighed and shook his head as though implying many of Archer's past conquests thought exactly the same. "Do you? Yes, he doesn't have a vampire heritage, which is a concern, but it's more than that. He's never committed to anyone, not one single woman. Why do you think he'll commit to you?"

His question, and what it suggested, pummeled every inch of her flesh, creating invisible but palpable damage. Battered and bruised her psyche. But why did it cause so much pain?

Because it rang true. And even though she knew Archer's stance, went into the arrangement fully aware, the reinforced realization sliced deep. "He understands us, our culture, and we have chemistry, synergy. Plus, Archer assured me he's ready to settle down." *At least for a few months.*

"If things don't go as planned, and there's a high probability they won't, have you thought about the fallout? There are potentially huge ramifications. It will impact on my friendship with him and possibly the business."

Her brother's negativity practically ripped out her heart. But, given the facts, she couldn't blame him. Not that she ideally wanted a short-term affair or could even hint at the truth. However, to meet her and Archer's needs, their sham remained the best solution.

No one else could know their full intentions. The more people they told, the greater the risk to their already precarious campaign. "And if our relationship works, it will have positive outcomes for me, your friendship with Archer and the company. A triple win."

Bror propped his elbows on his desk and leaned forward, a stern, disappointed expression on his face.

"What happened to finding a reliable, faithful man...
with vampire ancestry?"

She'd wondered whether he'd return to, and run
with, that old decaying chestnut. Up until now,
everyone in her family had married a partner with
varying degrees of vampire genetics.

"I never specified that. *You* did. My focus has always
been on finding love with a guy who is keen to commit
to me. Cultural background doesn't matter as long as
I'm aligned with my partner...mentally, emotionally,
sexually. The spark between Archer and me is the
strongest I've experienced with anyone." The absolute
truth.

"Lust connections are often fleeting, briefly burning
bright then fizzling out fast."

His words triggered a flood of raw emotion, but she
somehow quashed her reactive response. "You're
assuming what I have with Archer is one-dimensional,
purely fueled by physical drivers. It's not."

"Isn't it? You've only recently gotten together. Your
relationship is in its infancy, too early in its
development to be much else."

Since when had her single brother become a
relationship expert? "I suppose we'll just have to see.
There are always exceptions to rigid rules. Who knows?
Maybe in this case our chemistry is an indicator of a
soulmate connection." She wished.

"Let's hope. But unfortunately, given Archer's
history, the odds of what you have lasting longer than
a short fling aren't in your favor."

His statement may have some accuracy, but it was
also equally annoying. "Are you saying people can't
mature, change?"

"No. I'm saying he hasn't shown any behaviors that suggest he's progressed until this...thing with you. So I'm skeptical, wary, because I want the best for my baby sister, and I'm not convinced this new, improved version of him is sustainable. Believe me, if you truly care for him, I want it to work."

Really? She was doubtful, after his persistent attempts to turn her off Archer and, particularly, following his 'I thought you wanted to find a vampire partner' comment. "I'm not a baby anymore. I'm a grown woman, and I can make my own decisions."

Temperance snuck in a quick, resetting breath, and reined in her building frustration. "I appreciate your concern, but it's my life. You can't protect me from everything that could possibly go wrong. I need to give things a go, and part of that means I'll make mistakes, but that's what it takes to learn and grow."

This time he smiled with full sincerity. "You have grown up. Australia's been good for you."

"It really has." So far. She loved living in Melbourne, even before this eventuation with Archer. But now, her desire to stay had doubled.

"I honestly hope you're right about him, your relationship. I'd hate to see you crushed." He exhaled and shook his head, his gaze reconnecting with hers. "But you can count on me to help pick up the broken pieces."

He said it as if it were an absolute, foregone conclusion, as though he expected her heartbreak. "Bror!" He had a legitimate point, but for fuck's sake. She didn't need reminding of it.

"I just mean I'll be here for you, no matter what. I truly wish you both the best."

She hoped so. She hoped he didn't intend to cause trouble in the background to achieve the outcome *he* wanted, what *he* thought was best. "I'm happy to hear it. Then you shouldn't have any issues telling Archer you support us. Ready?"

"Now?"

"Yes." She fixed her firmest listen-to-me stare on him, peering right into his eyes. "Don't disconnect." First hurdle almost cleared.

Temperance rejoined Archer and handed over her phone. "My brother wants to say something."

Archer shot up into standing and discarded his mobile on the armrest of her couch. He lifted a questioning eyebrow at her, then focused on her phone screen. "Sort out everything with your sister?"

"For the moment. I'm hoping I won't have to put out a whole heap of spot fires that burn out of control into a raging inferno."

"You really did miss your calling as a writer."

"This isn't the time to fuck around. And I especially don't want you fucking around with my sister. Got it?" Bror stabbed his finger at the screen as though to punctuate his point. "Don't screw with her if you don't see a future. She's not a fling type of girl."

Temperance snatched her phone from Archer and glared at her brother. "You were supposed to tell him you support our relationship, not threaten him."

"I had to make sure he understood the conditions of my acceptance and endorsement."

She rolled her eyes and huffed out a frustrated breath.

Archer shifted into the frame beside her and ran a soothing hand slowly up and down her back. "I get it. I promise you we've both entered into this with full awareness. Even if there wasn't so much at stake, I would never take advantage. You know me. You know it's not my modus operandi.

"Temperance and I trust and respect each other and have agreed to be one-hundred percent transparent. Each relationship decision we make is done with thorough consultation and full consent. We're equals in this, every single step of the way. Does that put you at ease?"

Her brother's gaze flicked between them both as if to ensure she agreed with what Archer had said, that he'd fairly represented their situation. And she did, and he had, wholeheartedly. "Somewhat. You're great with words, you always have been. But will your actions back what you've said? That's what really counts. That's what will satisfy me as to whether you truly are serious about Temperance."

"Fair enough. I'd respond exactly the same way if our situations were reversed."

"Good. Then, we understand each other, so I shouldn't have any nasty surprises."

She hoped none of them did. "So are you guys done with all your male posturing, macho crap?"

Archer and her brother had the decency to look embarrassed.

"Thanks for calling to let me know about your new relationship status. Now go enjoy the rest of your night." He glared at Archer. "But not too much."

She groaned. "Bye, Bror." She pressed the 'end call' button before he could say anything else and dumped her phone on the dining table.

"That went well."

She pivoted in Archer's arms and pinned him with a raised-eyebrow stare.

"Whatever you said to him worked. He seemed to believe our story and come around to the idea of us as a couple. It's essential to have him onside, in case we have any issues with the visa. He can sincerely back and support our claim without the slightest bit of coercion."

All true. If Bror needed to answer questions about them, it was imperative he didn't come across as coached. He needed to sound sure, not compromised and conflicted. "I still can't believe my smart, confident, level-headed brother practically turned into a caveman."

"He lives far away and feels responsible for you. He's driven to do whatever it takes to protect you as best he can."

"But he's your friend, too. Like I told him, he needs to let go of the leash and recognize me as an adult, a grown woman who can make her own decisions. I love him, but he needs to stop trying to micro-manage me, stop being such a control freak and let me live my life."

"I think he might have gotten that point." Archer brushed the back of his knuckles over her cheek. "There's absolutely no denying you're a grown woman — and an incredibly sexy one."

"Thank you. But I imagine lust makes that a lot easier to see."

"And appreciate." He glided his hand gently down her back and over her butt, and pressed a soft, enticing kiss to her lips.

This man was mesmerizing, intoxicating. With him so close, every one of her senses went into overdrive. In his presence she struggled not to touch him, and when alone, she struggled to stop thinking about him, struggled to stop touching herself, almost burning through all her vibrator batteries. His hands-on behavior suggested he suffered with the same all-consuming, almost-obsessive affliction.

If she didn't slow things down, they'd be naked and writhing in minutes, which sounded amazing, incredible and dangerously tempting. Mustering every ounce of banked strength, she broke their lip lock. "You went a little Neanderthal, too, but overall, you were pretty great. Everything you said accurately represented our relationship."

"It did, as I promised. Outside of omitting some details regarding how we started seeing each other, I said no outright lies. And I'm assuming you didn't either." He cupped her ass, and tugged her against his steel-hard torso, his cock prodding her stomach.

What did he say? Her body's overwhelming response to him, her desperate need to come, had shut down her hearing and shunted all sensation along sensual pathways.

He'd proven his ability to take her to spectacular heights, and although she wanted him to do it again, first she needed to show her desire to reciprocate, which was far from a chore because she craved his cock. She'd imagined how he'd taste, how he'd look and sound when he came, ever since he went down on her in his home.

No, from much earlier. Almost from the instant they'd met. She'd just tried to ignore it, initially, thinking it'd cause issues, fantasizing about her brother's friend and business partner. Her boss. A usually forbidden circumstance on so many levels.

Temperance looped her arms around his neck, stood on tiptoes…and he took over, gripping her jaw, angling her face and crushing his lips to hers, delving his tongue deep.

She whimpered, grateful he held her so tight, or her unsteady legs would have buckled, dropping her to the floor.

Trailing her lips along his neck, she nipped and sucked, giving him a love bite, something to mark him as hers without converting him into a vampire. Just a playful, territorial nibble.

His raspy groan fed her enthusiasm, and she lifted his top over his head and threw it across the room. She kissed down his bare chest and stopped to lick and suck his nipples, subtly pushing him toward the couch. The backs of Archer's legs hit the edge of the seat and he dropped into sitting.

She kneeled between his thighs, unbuttoned his fly and *oh!* Commando. The man was full of surprises. Did he always hang loose and free? Even at work? The idea had her salivating and her core clenching.

Reaching into his jeans, she freed his cock and, goodness me, what a specimen—smooth and long, with just the right circumference, fitting perfectly in her grip. And he manscaped. No big unruly bush—a neatly trimmed thatch, the ideal licking and sucking conditions.

She ran her tongue over her lips—a reflex action—swallowed the inordinate amount of saliva in her mouth and swooped down, tonguing the head of his dick. *Clean, a little salty, a lot delicious.*

He grunted, gripped her head with both hands and held her mouth just out of reach of his steel-hard shaft. "You sure?"

"Very, very sure." She held his gaze, licked along the length of him and swirled her tongue over and around the end of his cock.

He grasped tighter, a zing of pain-pleasure spiking in her scalp. "Fuck me."

She couldn't wait...but she would. She had to. Only one more month or so.

In the meantime... "I want you to come in my mouth, Sir."

An unintelligible part-growl, part-groan rumbled from his throat. She pumped his cock in a coordinated rhythm, working him with her hand and lips and tongue until he hovered on the brink of release.

With his dick thick, engorged and ready to explode, she slowed things down, easing her grip and moving to give some special attention to his balls. She continued the pleasurable torture for a little longer, his increased grunts and thrusts plus the firm, hot feel of his fingers buried in her hair, dialing her own desire right back up to pre-climax.

Redirecting her mouth to his cock, she flicked her tongue over the sensitive underside, then licked off the pre-cum leaking from his slit. She recommenced the combined lick-suck-hand-pump combo, and he plunged between her lips, taking himself deeper, which she loved. Loved seeing him so out of control. So overtaken by pleasure. Pleasure she'd given him.

"I'm close." His rough, breathless voice gave her an additional warning, another opportunity to change her mind, which got her extra horny.

She doubled her speed and sucking intensity, and he came with a roar, shooting jets of cum into her mouth, down her throat. And she swallowed everything he gave her.

He collapsed against the backrest, dropped his hands from her head, his breathing coming hard and fast. "Fucking incredible."

She skimmed her palms along his legs and peppered kisses on his inner thighs. Before she could even think of shifting out of kneeling, he sat forward and lifted her onto his lap. "Your turn."

Chapter Ten

Two weeks later, Temperance had almost moved into Archer's house. She stopped by her apartment briefly after work to collect her mail, some toiletries and extra clothes.

He'd asked her to pack a sexy dress because he'd arranged to take her out tonight. He didn't say where or what for, and she couldn't wait to find out. She'd always loved surprises.

Overnight bag slung over her arm, she returned to her car and stopped. Using her key fob, she unlocked the doors and subtly scanned the area. She could have sworn she felt someone's eyes on her, but no one stood out. Maybe just nerves? Uncertainty?

She got into the driver's seat and traveled the familiar route to Archer's place—what had quickly become her second home. From what she could see, no one had followed her. She hated to be paranoid, but she couldn't discount her innate Jade-Violet senses—the vampire equivalent of a gut feeling.

She refocused on the road ahead. Up until this evening, Archer had either cooked dinner or they'd ordered in, and afterward they'd spent the rest of the night indulging in each other and working off all the calories they'd ingested.

The best, most enjoyable exercise she'd ever done. And going by their continued enthusiasm to get down and dirty, the lust showed no signs of waning, not even a hint of dissipating. Quite the opposite.

Their physical exploits had revealed bits and pieces of each other, but they had forged an unspoken agreement to hold off on stripping bare. It kept things fresh, exciting and inventive…like extended foreplay.

He'd worked her with her vibrator and added his mouth and hands to the stimulation. The result? She'd come harder and faster than ever before and almost blacked out. She'd dipped in and out of consciousness for several minutes, floating on a cloud of full-blown bliss.

Temperance reached the traffic lights a block from his house, already turned on, her pussy ridiculously wet, and hardly remembered the last half of the trip, her mind overrun with images of their intimate time together, the way he made her feel, what he had planned for the night ahead.

She parked on the street in front of his place, and he greeted her at the door wearing impeccably fitted trousers, his shirt unbuttoned and the sleeves rolled up, giving her a great glimpse of his gorgeous chest and abs and arms. Without a word, he hauled her inside for a passionate kiss.

With their growing compulsion to keep touching one another, she predicted they'd be fully naked soon, maybe by the end of the evening, adding to the thrill of anticipation.

Archer grabbed her overnight bag and slung it over his shoulder, his eyes sparkling with mischief. She'd grown to know that look all too well. "Wait here. I've got something for you," he said, and disappeared down the corridor.

Another surprise? From the moment he'd suggested this scheme, he'd done nothing but spoil her. Were his actions an indicator of what a real relationship with the man would look like? Could he sustain this level of attentive behavior? Could she? "What time do I need to be ready?" she called out.

Archer returned with a wicked smile and carried something behind his back. "The sooner the better." He waved a hand toward the couch. "But first, take a seat."

She did, and he sat beside her, their closest knees rubbing. "What are you hiding?"

"You mean this?" He brought his other hand forward, unfurled his fingers and revealed a mini black vibrator and wireless remote control. "I want you to wear it tonight."

"Tonight? And let me guess, you have total control of the remote."

"Spot on, baby."

"What if someone...notices?"

"It's all part of the fun. Can you keep quiet, sit still and enjoy the pleasure with others around?"

She smacked his arm. "You're evil! You know I'm a moaner, a squirmer. I've got no chance of passing this...test."

"You might surprise yourself." He pressed a whisper of a kiss to her lips. A prelude, a promise of more to come later.

"Whatever happens, I'll enjoy watching you." He put the remote in the front pocket of his pants and handed her the vibrator. "Go get ready and, when you're done, insert the bullet, and rejoin me."

Oh God! Hopefully he didn't intend to take her anywhere too busy. Actually, bustling would be better than quiet...unless they were alone. But he hadn't given her any details, which increased her anxiety, yet got her all-the-more horny.

She showered and slipped into her cleavage-enhancing violet A-line dress, her mind buzzing with thoughts of possible scenarios, then slid the cool bullet into place, followed by her see-through black-and-purple panties.

"Ready?"

She startled and spun in the direction of his voice. Archer stood in the bedroom doorway, his shoulder propped against the doorframe, his arms crossed, looking super suave and sophisticated.

He'd left the top few buttons of his shirt open — providing a teasing glimpse of his broad chest — and secured the cuffs with platinum-and-black cufflinks, his black suit cut perfectly to conform to his body. A breathtaking male specimen... And he was all hers, at least for a few more weeks.

She tried not to drool. "Almost. What's the special occasion?"

"Can't I treat my girlfriend to a night out?"

"That didn't exactly answer my question."

"And that didn't exactly answer mine." He raised an eyebrow, a triumphant smile on his handsome face.

Her brother was right. Archer excelled at words, and their usage. "Fine. Yes, you can. In fact, I encourage it."

"Thank you." He smiled with one-hundred-percent sincerity. "Honestly, I wanted to show you off, be seen together around town, take some more pictures and clips of us enjoying ourselves. Well, the G-rated version."

Of course. How could she forget? He wasn't doing this specifically for her. They had a story to sell. Her misguided enthusiasm deflated like a popped balloon, leaking air.

Although they got on great in every aspect of their lives so far, she couldn't delude herself into believing their relationship would necessarily transition to something real, substantial — something committed and long-term.

She could wish as much as she wanted, but he needed to agree. He needed to acknowledge serious feelings for her if they had any chance of long-lasting success.

Temperance detoured to her refilled overnight bag and rummaged through it until she found what she needed. She slipped into black patent leather pumps, her legs a little shaky, grabbed her matching purse and selected a shawl in case it got cool.

Archer roved his eyes over her, lingering on her breasts then traveling up to meet her gaze. Her nipples beaded as though physically caressed and begging for more. "You look stunning."

He prowled toward her, clasped her hand and interlinked their fingers. "We'd better go before I rip off your dress, throw you onto the bed and devour you instead."

Was that supposed to hurry her along, because it did the exact opposite? But pride and determination, in conjunction with curiosity, drove her forward. She could find out what Archer was up to, and they could indulge later…within her clearly set parameters.

They made it to his SUV, and the second she clicked her seatbelt into place, a gentle buzz started up in her sex. She jumped and sucked in a stilted breath.

Before she could get a handle on the weird yet titillating sensation, the car engine roared to life, adding additional vibration to her clit. He only had to drive over a speed hump, and she'd come for sure.

"All right?" Archer studied her from the driver's seat, a smirk on his face.

"If on the verge of free-falling into an orgasm is all right, then *yes*."

"Mmm…right where I want you."

She dug her fingers into her thighs, trying to stave off coming too soon. Archer pressed his palm to the back of her closest hand, comforting, assuring, arousing. A vow. "We're going to have so much fun tonight."

Like they hadn't since they'd embarked on this fake-dating journey.

They drove into Williamstown, chatting the whole way, and miraculously avoided any significant bumps, distracting her from the party in her pussy. He parked near a fancy restaurant with fairy lights, overlooking the ocean, and she stifled a *squee*. The venue, the location, encompassed everything she loved.

Maybe she should have tapped into her body's heightened state of arousal and given herself some relief before they arrived. Because she didn't, she'd have to suffer with the unrelenting ache and frustration all through dinner. If he let her, which, no doubt, he wouldn't, upping the coming criteria until she shattered.

He wouldn't dare torment her with the different vibration settings while surrounded by other people in public though, would he? Risk her gasps and moans of pleasure as she came? His earlier comments had to have been a joke, something to add additional spice to their encounter. Didn't they?

She got out of the car on wobbly legs and absorbed the surroundings. The whiff of scrumptious food, tinged with salty sea air, made her stomach growl, and the sun dipping toward the horizon created a spectacular sky streaked with gold, orange, pink and purple. Soft music mixed with the hum of people's chatter, and the roar and crash of the waves added to the amazing atmosphere.

Archer joined her on the passenger side and threaded their fingers together. "What do you think?"

"It's beautiful. Perfect." As though he'd dived into her thoughts and recreated her number one definition of romance.

"Yeah, it's a special spot." He gave her hand a gentle tug. "Let's go in."

The moment they entered, one of the wait staff ushered them to a private dining room with a magnificent wall of windows overlooking the beach.

"I'll be your server tonight." The waiter seated them both and gestured to the menus on the table. "I'll leave you for a few minutes to decide on some drinks."

She snatched up her menu, eager to choose what to order, so she could go snuggle with Archer by the window and admire the view.

She should probably select seafood and a white wine, given the setting, but she couldn't go past the carpaccio raw steak dish, followed by the Pittsburgh rare steak, and a glass or two of red. "What did you dec—?"

Archer was no longer in his chair. He'd dropped to one knee, right beside her.

She gasped, slamming her hand to her mouth.

"I wondered how long it would take for you to notice me."

How long? She could tell him exactly how long...immediately, from the instant her eyes had clapped onto him, prior to them being officially introduced. His potent presence and delectable good looks were impossible to ignore.

Before she could summon any intelligible speech, he flipped open the ring box in his outstretched hand. She couldn't stop staring at the elegant platinum ring, and especially the large, sparkling purple diamond. "Marry me in two weeks?"

Temperance stared at him and blinked, blinked again, as though disbelieving the picture in front of her. But Archer remained on one knee, open ring box in hand, waiting.

She hadn't expected him to buy an expensive engagement ring and actually propose. Maybe the guy literally had more money than sense. "I didn't... I thought... I, um... I figured you'd just give it to me."

His lips curved into a sinful grin. "Oh, and I will. Good and hard...if you say *yes*."

She squeezed her thighs together, the steady internal buzz pressing right against a pleasure point. A breathy whimper escaped her lips.

"Is that a *yes*?" Mischief danced in his devilish eyes.

It'd become a *yes, yes yes!* if she didn't assert some control over her hedonistic body. "I thought we'd already agreed."

"We had, but...I wanted to check you hadn't changed your mind — and get some great proposal pics to add to our evidence base."

His response snuffed out her flare of hope — that his effort to propose might mean more. A forced, I'm-all-in smile twitched on her lips. "I haven't changed my mind."

"Good." He removed the ring, put the small box on the table, grasped her left hand and slid the striking solitaire onto her finger. "It suits you. I knew it would the moment I saw it."

"You went ring shopping?"

"Mostly online. I narrowed down the choices then checked them out in person. This one spoke to me." He lifted her hand to his lips and kissed each knuckle, slowly, reverently, lingering on her ring finger. "It reminded me of you — rare, precious, beautiful."

Wow. He didn't need to say that. This whole thing was fake, a means to a hopefully mutually satisfying end — nothing to do with their 'romance' — so why bother?

He didn't need to try to win her over. They'd both agreed to the terms of their arrangement. She'd give herself fully to him once they wed and engage in a lot of other fun in the meantime.

Maybe he wanted to make sure she wouldn't change her mind before he could thoroughly sample every bit of her? He had no worries. She wouldn't walk away without fully experiencing him, either.

A ray of sunlight reflected off the dazzling diamond. She still couldn't believe the ring fit so perfectly, like Cinderella's slipper. Except their story wasn't a fairy tale.

Its trajectory suggested the opposite of a happy ending. He could use the prettiest words in the world, but they didn't equate to forever love. She needed to keep reminding her dreamy, romantic self of that fact.

"Thank you. It's lovely." She angled her finger, the diamond facets catching more light and reflecting a kaleidoscope of colors across the walls, the ceiling, the long white tablecloth.

Archer grabbed his phone out of his inside jacket pocket, held her be-ringed hand and snapped some pics. He reviewed them and glanced at her with a big, broad smile. "Gorgeous."

He shifted his seat right beside hers and put his arm around her. "Couple selfie time."

They squished in tight together, and he took some more photos of them smiling, laughing.

"Do you need a few more minutes?"

The amorous bubble burst, and she darted her gaze up to find their server standing beside the table. How had he snuck in so quietly? She had to keep that in mind. The man had ninja stealth.

Normally she detected the distinctive human scent the moment one of them entered her space. However, she'd been wrapped up in her fake fiancé's unexpectedly romantic proposal, plus his overwhelming pheromones and physical presence.

Archer shifted impossibly closer and kissed her temple. "A bottle of your best champagne, please."

"Yes, Sir. A special occasion?"

"Indeed. We just got engaged."

"Congratulations." The server looked suitably sincere, his smile reaching his eyes. "Would you like me to take some photos?"

"Let's do that when you return with the champagne."

The moment the waiter left the room, Archer cupped her face with one hand and took her lips in a heated kiss. "This engagement thing is much more enjoyable than I realized."

"And the night has only just started."

"Exactly." Balls of blue fire ignited in his eyes. She'd seen it numerous times now. The shade signified he had some sensual scenarios in store. A shiver spiraled up her spine at the earth-shattering possibilities.

Their waiter returned with the bottle of sparkling wine nestled in an ice bucket, and two champagne flutes. He popped the cork, making her jump, and poured them each a glass.

Archer handed his phone to the guy. "Snap away." With his magnificent, mega-watt smile in place, Archer held her plastered to his side, his glass raised. She snuggled in, her smile matching his, and lifted her glass to show off her engagement ring.

After the server took several shots, her fake fiancé angled himself toward her and tapped his flute to hers. "To us." The panty-stripping potency in his tone had her toes curling in her pumps.

They each had a sip, set their glasses on the table, and kissed. Slow, tender, loving... For anyone watching, they'd believe the show, maybe because only one of them was acting.

Every interaction with Archer, she infused with passion, desire, love. It just happened. She could censor her feelings verbally, but not physically. Each time they touched, her emotions leaked through the connection, like blood through a bite.

"Here you go, Sir."

Her brain jolted back to the present, and she broke the intoxicating kiss. They weren't at home. They weren't alone.

The waiter went to hand over Archer's phone, but all of Archer's attention was focused on her, as though she'd cast a spell on him. And maybe she had, via some special sequence in her vampire DNA. She accepted his mobile and smiled.

"Have you had a chance to choose some food?" In other words, had they been too busy devouring each other to decide?

She met Archer's penetrating stare. "Do you know what you want?"

"I sure do." His gaze traveled over her body and settled on her face. "Do you?"

Oh yes, more of him. But instead of saying anything, she revisited the range of dinner choices, sticking with her original decision. "The carpaccio for my entrée, and the Pittsburgh rare steak for my main, please."

Without even attempting to read a menu, Archer rattled off his two selections, and the waiter left to place their orders.

They reviewed the fantastic pictures and video the guy had taken. She and Archer looked believably overjoyed and ecstatic, like a smitten couple ready to take the next step, a couple eager to share their life together.

"Consider these added to our growing evidence folder." He placed his phone face-down on the table. "No more interruptions until our food arrives." Archer removed the remote from his pants pocket, his thumb poised over the selector button. "Let's play."

Chapter Eleven

"Now? But the waiter could walk back in any minute."

Archer pressed the button once, twice. "Adds to the thrill, don't you think?"

The vibration intensity and speed tripled, leaving her wide-eyed and speechless — but not moanless. She clamped her jaw together, which only slightly dampened her persistent little cries of pleasure. *Damn him!* This was agonizingly delightful.

"You look so fucking beautiful." He nuzzled her neck, and slowly slid his hand up and down her inner thigh, not quite reaching her clit.

She spread her legs wide, like a wanton, desperate woman.

"I want to watch you come," he said, his voice a low growl. "Right here. Right now." Archer closed the distance to her clit with his fingers and stroked.

She climaxed instantly, burying her face in his shoulder to muffle her scream.

"That's it, baby. Come all over my hand."

He helped her wring out every last drop, and she slumped against him, still panting. The orgasm haze soon started to lift, and reality slammed back into her brain. They were in a restaurant, their first courses due any minute. Or had they already come?

Temperance broke their intimate embrace and swung her gaze across the table. Thank the universe, no food had arrived during her incredibly enjoyable lapse in judgment.

"How was that?" Archer kept his eyes on her and adjusted the vibration down a notch.

"You're a wicked, wicked man."

"Looks like you *really* enjoy wicked."

She glared at him, even though he'd hit the nail on the captain-obvious head.

Their meals arrived less than a minute after she roused from her post-climax bliss bubble. So close to getting caught. And yet a bolt of excitement struck deep in her pussy.

Once their entrée plates were collected, the second course came quickly. They chatted and ate, with no more close calls, Archer acting like the perfect gentleman. So why did her stomach flutter with warning? The handsome, eloquent man had to have something else hidden up his perfectly smoothed sleeve, brewing in his sexually deviant mind.

Archer mopped his mouth with his white cloth napkin. "Would you like some dessert?"

"Are you kidding? We just finished our mains." She lightly pressed her palm to her distended stomach and rubbed. "I'm about to burst."

"Well, I definitely need my dessert fix."

The server appeared and loaded up their empty dishes. "How was everything?"

Everything had been brilliant—the food, the company, the outstanding orgasm.

"Excellent. Beyond expectation."

She couldn't agree more with Archer's summary of the evening so far.

"Thank you, Sir. I'll feed that back to the chef."

"We will have dessert and coffee but would like a bit of break first."

"No problem at all. I'll check in with you in twenty minutes?"

"Great."

The door clicked shut behind the departing waiter, and Archer focused his rakish eyes on hers. "Party time."

"Pardon?"

"I'm an impatient man when I know what I want." He brushed a kiss to her lips and disappeared beneath the table.

"W-what are you doing?"

"Eating dessert early."

"But what if—?"

"We've got nineteen minutes to play. And I need to taste my fiancée." He ran the tip of his nose along her inner thigh.

"Archer!" She lifted the long white tablecloth so she could see his incorrigible face.

"Let me have a lick." His warm breath caressed her clit. "Tell me you don't want it." Confidence radiated from his eyes, his tone.

"I don't want it."

"Yeah, ah...you might want to try again, this time with some conviction." He raised his eyebrows and stared at her, silently asking her to defy his assumption.

"Okay, I want it, but not here. After. We can celebrate after."

"Relax. If the waiter returns, he'll think I've gone to the restroom." He pushed her dress up to her hips and hooked a couple of fingers into the top of her panties. "Be a good girl and take these off."

"Archer!"

"Come on. Think about how good I can make you feel."

Reason warred with desire.

And desire won. "Fine. But be quick," she said in a you're-an-arrogant-annoying-man tone.

"That's up to you, baby." He chuckled.

She glared at her infuriatingly hot, fake fiancé, but let him help her shimmy out of her underwear and shift forward on the seat. He tucked the scrap of lace into his chest pocket like a prize.

"You can't leave my undies *there*. No one will believe they're a pocket handkerchief."

"You can't control what people think. They'll believe whatever they want to believe." He trailed his knuckles lightly over her folds, sending tingles rippling through her core. "Stop worrying about what may or may not happen and enjoy the moment."

Temperance folded the edge of the tablecloth onto the table and pinned it in place with a glass so she could continue to watch him. And she kept her dress out of the way to give him unobstructed access.

He stared at her bare, pale-skinned pussy as though it were a work of art, like he couldn't ever get sick of admiring, smelling, touching, tasting every millimeter of her skin.

"Mmm…gorgeous." He let out a semi-pained groan, then kissed a slow, elaborate path to her pussy, as though he honestly didn't care if they got discovered or what anyone thought but her. And that was both frustrating and inconceivably flattering.

She shamelessly spread her legs wider, and thrust into his face, seeking extra friction.

"Mmm...I want to feast on you." He took her up on her bold invitation and delved in deeper, teasing her clit with his tongue and taking her right to the brink.

"Please!" she whisper-pleaded, her body trembling. "Hurry."

She gripped his head with one hand, angling his mouth right where she wanted him and ground against his super-skilled tongue, her hushed erratic moans becoming harder and harder to control.

"Best thing I've eaten all day," he said, and went to town, licking and sucking until she shattered. Not just a regular orgasm — an incredibly powerful climax, enhanced by the bullet's persistent vibration, and partly fueled by adrenaline at the idea of being caught.

Every ounce of tension drained from her body, leaving her boneless and sated. The all-consuming relaxation almost had her slipping off the seat to join Archer under the table. Speaking of the mischievous man, he massaged the accessible swell of her bottom and dotted soft, moist kisses over her inner thighs.

Sweat beaded between her breasts and trickled onto her stomach. She fanned her face with her hand, and the waiter re-entered the room. Had twenty minutes passed already? Time really did fly when having fun. Her eyes widened, and she shoved the glass aside, dropping the tablecloth over her lap to cover Archer's head, trying not to look guilty.

Temperance sat up straight and attempted to tug her dress down, but Archer ensured she kept her pussy bared to him, brazenly repositioning his lips at the apex of her legs and flicking her clit sporadically with his tongue.

She swallowed a moan, and tried for an innocent, everything's-lovely smile.

The waiter's gaze caught on her cheeks. "You look flushed. Is it too hot in here? I can adjust the thermostat."

"I'm fine, thank you. It's probably the wine." *And Archer's incredibly attentive, sinful mouth.*

The internal buzzy sensation suddenly shot up, and she struggled to sit still. The bastard had fiddled with the bullet levels and ramped up the vibration.

Later, she'd make Archer pay for his antics, in the most torturously pleasurable way. While he facilitated an orgasm frenzy, she'd do the opposite. Tease and extend out the foreplay as long as possible before allowing him to come. Or, depending on her mood, she might stick with orgasm denial.

"Did you decide what you'd like for dessert?"

Archer's mouth pressed against her mound, muffling his low chuckle.

"U-um, y-es." Focus. Concentrate. She could do this...without coming in the server's presence. The tingly ache in her pelvis grew exponentially, yet miraculously she ordered them the charcuterie board and some coffees, without another hitch in her speech.

The door clicked closed behind the waiter, and she climaxed...again. The wondrous relief spiraled through her like a rapturous whirlwind.

She opened her eyes to find Archer peeking from under the tablecloth. "I'm assuming the coast is clear," he said with a roguish grin.

Without waiting for her answer — *cocky bastard* — he emerged from beneath the table, smoothed out his slightly crumpled suit and returned to his spot right beside her. He raked a hand through his tousled hair to tame it down and planted a super-hot kiss on her lips. "You are so fucking sexy...and fun. So much fun."

She wanted to be angry at Archer for putting her in such a precarious position but couldn't muster up the energy, not after he'd given her such high praise and an accompanying thrilling experience.

He leaned into her ear, his breath hot with promise. "I can't want to get you home."

Home.

His home.

A temporary stop on her relationship journey.

If only he meant *home* in a long-term-commitment capacity. In line with her definition, her fantasy, her dream.

However, she knew what she was getting into with him. He'd made the situation more than clear regarding his aims and intentions. How it would benefit them both.

How they could maximize their time and enhance their enjoyment together. And she had agreed. Not once had he led her on. He'd been nothing but transparent — and a total sex god. So she couldn't complain.

If she sensed a deeper connection when they interacted, it came through her skewed, wishful view, her desire-driven lens. And unless he said something different, she had to presume he'd chosen to stick to the terms of their original plan.

Both of them had the right and ability to end their arrangement at their discretion. Both of them had a choice in whether the circumstances continued to meet their needs. So, at some point, she'd have to evaluate how long she was willing to live in a faux marriage.

How long was she willing to stay out of the dating scene and put the possibility of a real relationship on the backburner? Because she wanted to meet her soulmate and start a family.

"Temperance? You still with me?" His rich, sensual voice pulled her out of her head and back into the present.

His breathtaking blue eyes scrutinized hers, as though attempting to read the truth behind her forced neutral facade. What would he say if he knew she harbored serious feelings for him? Would he deem their 'courtship' too complicated and call the whole thing off? "If you behave."

He raised an incredulous eyebrow. "I don't think so. You may protest, initially, but the true you, your essence, loves naughty. Attracts it. Vanilla isn't for you. Too boring. You need excitement."

"Sure you're not talking about yourself?"

"I'm talking about you and me and why we work, sexually. Why we have such explosive energy. Synergy."

And how about the rest? The non-physical. "What about outside of that?"

"If we didn't have a level of friendship, intellectual stimulation and mutual respect, we couldn't do this. We'd drive each other nuts. Sexual compatibility only gets you so far. There's a lot of time we need to spend together in between, and if it's not amicable, the rest goes to shit. If we piss each other off, the last thing we'll want to do is touch."

Weren't they the key elements of a successful relationship? The kind of traits that highlighted the person as a suitable partner? What secret ingredient did he require to consider someone seriously? And more importantly, did she possess it?

The charcuterie board came with their coffees, breaking the conversational flow. She would have to steer the discussion back in this direction at another point and try to discover what would get him over the commitment line.

Chapter Twelve

Bordering on a cheese coma but high on Temperance, Archer linked her arm through his and strolled back to the car. A massive effort, given he craved more of her, wanted to press her up against the closest wall and make sure she fully committed to being his — for the duration of their time together, anyway.

A moan sliced through the dark, quiet night. "Sounds like they're having as good a time as we did." And he planned to continue the party when they got back to his place.

Instead of laughing along with him, she stiffened, her gaze zeroing in on a silhouetted couple in the distance. She broke out of his embrace and bolted.

"Temperance?" He grabbed her windswept shawl before it hit the ground, shoved it into an inside jacket pocket and took off after her but couldn't keep up. *What the fuck?*

A few hundred meters ahead, one of the couple ran off, and the other crumpled to the ground.

"Call zero-zero-one!" Temperance shouted, dropping to her knees.

The vampire-staffed ambulance number. *Fuck.* He stopped, his breath shunting in and out of his lungs, whipped his phone from his pocket and dialed.

The call center answered, and he reported the scant details, along with the address coordinates, and made his way to meet up with his fiancée...and an injured, unconscious full-human man, who could have been his doppelganger.

Not to sound paranoid, but had Archer been the true target? Two puncture wounds in the guy's neck oozed blood, and he shook uncontrollably. Archer shuddered and slammed a hand to the throbbing, accelerated pulse in his own throat.

Temperance cradled the victim's upper body and fixed her troubled gaze on Archer's eyes. "If I'd gotten here a minute later, he'd be dead."

He kneeled beside her, tried to stop trembling, and touched her shoulder. "But you didn't."

"He's not in the clear yet. If the ambulance doesn't get here in the next five minutes, he'll either die or be permanently changed."

Fuck. The news reported the odd vampire attack, the occasional turning, but he'd assumed it happened in less-affluent suburbs. Not that that was acceptable, none of it was, but he'd thought he wouldn't come across it in well-populated, 'safer' areas.

How much had the media hidden? How often did these kinds of attacks occur? Were they more prevalent than the news led people to believe? Most likely. If the media ran like any successful business, they'd promote what sold, flog the current agenda, what interested the masses...without sending them into an uncontrollable panic.

No time to get lost in unfounded fear, cynicism, conspiracy. He needed to remain focused, present, supportive...responsive.

Sirens sounded close by, getting louder by the second.

He met her worried gaze. "Did you get a look at the attacker?"

"Vaguely. Male. Obviously one with some sort of vampire genealogy. I couldn't tell what clan." She kept her palm pressed firmly over the patient's neck wound, trying to stem the bleeding, her hand covered in blood that looked as black as spilled oil in the moonlight.

Not a hint of hunger flared in her eyes, and yet he imagined seeing, feeling, smelling all that tempting blood had to tap into her survival instincts. She was one admirable, upstanding, in-control woman. Even in all this turmoil, it proved her altruism, her discipline, and added to her sexiness.

The ambulance screeched to an ear-splitting halt in a parking bay close to their spot on the sand. They wheeled out a stretcher and raced to their side on the beach. The hybrid vampire paramedics asked some questions about what had happened and any changes in the man's condition since Temperance had arrived, which she answered without hesitation.

Then the ambulance officers instructed them to move aside while they took over and tended to the guy's wounds and general health and wellbeing.

They injected the victim with vampire anti-venom, bandaged his neck, lifted him onto the stretcher and loaded him into the ambulance.

The male paramedic hopped into the driver's seat, while the female came to speak to them. "He's stable, but we'll take him to the closest available public hospital for further monitoring."

Temperance cuddled tight into Archer's side. "Thank you."

"Thank *you*. If you hadn't intervened, his chance of surviving would have been significantly reduced." She smiled, then jumped into the back of the ambulance with the patient, shut the doors and the vehicle drove off.

Archer kissed the top of Temperance's head and gave her a gentle squeeze. "Let's go get cleaned up."

She broke out of his arms and stared in horror at her bloodied hand and clothes, and his blood-spattered shirt and jacket. "I'm so sorry."

"About what? Saving a man's life?" Had she noticed the guy's scarily similar resemblance to him or had she been fully focused on the practicalities and attempting to stave off shock? No point raising it now — it'd only add to her stress and delay her recovery. Chances were it was just some freaky coincidence.

"Of course not. I mean, messing you up. Messing up such a wonderful night."

"You didn't mess up anything. Quite the contrary."

She pinched her eyebrows together, as if confused, as if not believing he could see the outcome of the evening as a positive.

"Come on." He grasped her non-blood-soaked hand and steered her toward his car. Once inside, he handed her some disinfectant wipes and a plastic bag to dispose of the rubbish to tide her over until she could scrub down in the shower at home.

His house. He shouldn't confuse the two terms, use them interchangeably. Yes, they shared a space, practically lived together, but that suited their current purposes. Nothing more. Right?

A requirement to increase their chances of achieving the best result. And yeah, okay, on a lust level, she shot the lights out. He couldn't deny the facts.

Best fucking all-around sexual experience he'd had with any woman. And they hadn't even had penetrative sex...yet. Whether the indescribably intense attraction, almost-addiction, continued, who knew? But he planned to make the most of their cohabitation while it lasted.

With the flood of adrenaline still fueling his system, Archer couldn't get home quickly enough, driving as fast as legally possible. On the way, he gave Temperance some space and speed dialed his lawyer, leaving a voicemail message with the news of their engagement, as promised.

Archer glanced over at his now-fiancée. He'd had his hands and mouth on Temperance for a high percentage of their dinner date, yet wanted more. Needed more.

More of her laughter, more of her company, more of her body. But only if she was up to interacting. After the trauma of what she'd just experienced, she may want to wash off the stress of the evening and crash.

And he'd support whatever she required.

They had tonight, and hopefully many more nights, to celebrate taking things further. Getting engaged and experiencing challenging situations together was new for both of them. An opportunity to share more of each other. Intimacy bred intimacy — as long as it didn't lead to an unrealistic expectation for a lifelong romance.

He parked in the garage, the roller door closing as he rushed to the passenger side. He whipped open her door, and she turned to him with a shy, self-conscious smile.

"Baby, stop overthinking. You were incredible tonight—with me, under pressure in unexpected circumstances."

"Then why do I feel so…inadequate."

Archer unclipped her seatbelt, whisked her into his arms and carried her inside. "I'm going to get us sorted then we're going to talk."

In the en suite, he turned on the shower, stripped them both out of their clothes and she removed the bullet. He cleaned it under the pounding water pressure, put it aside and held her to him underneath the steady stream of warm water.

Tonight was the first time they'd been fully naked together. Oh, he'd seen her whole delectable body, but in teasing little snippets…until now.

Fuck, she was beautiful, sexy, alluring. Bewitching. Caring, selfless, smart. Normally, his interest toward his woman-of-the-moment would have waned.

Maybe his lust-meter continued to fire on all fully juiced-up cylinders because he and Temperance hadn't done the deed. That, and he obviously had a thing for sweet, intelligent, honorable women.

Once they broke the final physical barrier, would his craving for her and her alone subside? How about her desire for him? Because, at the moment, the energy bouncing between them felt reciprocal. Equally as potent. The air around them virtually thrummed, ignited when in each other's presence.

He squirted some shower gel into his hand, sudsed it up, and slowly, gently massaged the foamy solution into her silky skin. No protest. One hundred percent trusting acquiescence.

Fuck, she blitzed his brain and made him revert to his primeval roots, tapped him into his baser self. Stroked his ego like rubbing a magic lamp and setting his inner Dom free.

Would he grant her three wishes? Oh yeah, and so many more…if she consented. Well, all except one. He couldn't do the commitment thing. That was where he drew the relationship line.

Almost for as long as he could remember, he refused to recreate his parents' stifled, resentful shotgun marriage. So, unsurprisingly, he'd never in his life shown a propensity to settle down. Given his strong stance, he couldn't guarantee a committed lifestyle, and he wouldn't lead women on.

He lathered himself up, scrubbing hard, then rinsed them both off, but stayed beneath the spray, as though hosing off the stress of the day, the stress of his wandering thoughts.

If women didn't like what he had to say, they were under no obligation to stick around. His dating history proved an abundance of like-minded, short-term, fun-focused women existed. So, why did his heart retaliate when he even thought about moving on from Temperance?

Because he enjoyed spending time with her beyond the sexual. A fucking first.

She wrapped her arms around his neck and snuggled in. Usually he'd consider that too clingy…in every sense. Too comfortable, setting off commitment alarm bells in his head and sending him into an I-need-to-escape-now flight response.

Except, instead of emotionally and physically fleeing, Archer turned off the taps, dried him and her with fluffy, absorbent bath sheets and entered his bedroom, his voice command activating the bedside lamps. He threw his fiancée onto the mattress, ready to ravage her and distract himself from his bewildering thoughts. Hers, too.

She bounced on the bed, a shocked, breathy laugh bursting out of her — so good to hear — her sweet pussy on display. His for the licking, the sucking, the stroking.

Oh yeah, this was what he needed — to focus on sating his voracious hunger. And hers too. Not some confounding, deep-and-meaningful dive into his emotions.

Tonight was about acknowledging and appreciating Temperance's worth, and extolling their official partnership, even though it had a fleeting future, an expiration date.

Archer raked his gaze slowly from her delicate feet all the way to her entrancing eyes.

She sat up, transfixed, her gaze traveling all over him as though wanting to catalog every little detail. And fuck, did his dick enjoy the attention, engorging until it hit his abs. Her pupils turned her spectacular eyes shiny onyx black, and she swiped her tongue over her lips, making them glisten.

He pressed her back to the mattress and followed her down, taking her lips in a scorching kiss, his cock sandwiched between their torsos, the friction driving him to the brink of blowing. But he had other plans for the way he wanted to come.

In tandem with Temperance.

Archer rolled over so she straddled him, her hair flowing freely over her shoulders like a delicate veil, her nipples grazing his chest. He could stare at her all night, except his pre-cum-covered cock urged him on.

"Turn around. I want your gorgeous pussy in my face, and your mouth aligned with my dick."

His clear command seemed to be exactly what she needed, and she scrambled into position. And, whoa, what a view. Add a mirrored ceiling and, fuck, exceptional. He really needed to rectify the situation and do the required renovation as soon as possible to make the most of every minute with his soon-to-be, scrumptious, short-term wife.

He spread her ass cheeks and licked from her clit to her rear hole. She gasp-moaned and sucked his cock from tip to base, the swirl and suction sending him too close to the finish line. He needed to triple his efforts if he wanted them to cross it together.

So he called on his A-plus game — rimming her back hole while simultaneously finger-fucking her pussy. When her juices started to flow, drenching his hand, he slid his fingers forward and circled her clit slowly, firmly. Then he changed it up suddenly and rubbed hard.

She came on his palm, her loud groan reverberating around his cock, setting off his own seismic climax.

They simultaneously rode out their mutual orgasms, exactly as he'd hoped. She collapsed atop him, and he slapped her ass.

Ow!" Temperance whipped her head around and glared at him.

She went to rub her butt to soothe the sting, but he grabbed her hand, held it behind her back, and grinned. "Don't act like you don't like it."

She squirmed, trying to break free of his hold. No chance. Not even with her Jade-Violet vampire genetics. He spanked both ass cheeks, turning them a glowing ruby red.

"Archer!" She wriggled and bucked — and descended into laughter.

"Admit you enjoy me taking control, and I'll let you go."

"You're unbelievable!" She couldn't hide her smile.

"So I've been told."

She groaned, and dropped her head onto his pelvis, but didn't concede.

As a test, he slightly loosened his grip, and surprise, fucking surprise, she thrust back with force, as anticipated. He gripped tighter and landed a few more slaps on her butt and the back of her thighs.

"All right. Enough. I surrender." She stopped thrashing, her breath pelting against his thigh.

Was she letting him win? Who knew? But, going by her responses, she got off on the game as much as he did.

"What do you need to say?"

"I enjoy it, okay?"

"Enjoy what, exactly?" Because, yeah, he was a bastard and wanted to hear her admit what she liked in detail.

She huffed and made a little sound of protest.

He waited, giving her space to collect her thoughts and see if she'd follow through.

She sighed. "You taking control. The way you touch me, kiss me, make me come. When you restrain me, spank me. When you talk dirty. Even spending non-sexual time together."

Him, too. The fantastic sexual connection wasn't a surprise, going by their off-the-charts chemistry. But the way they interacted outside of the bedroom, how comfortable yet aroused she made him feel, consistently, with the intensity growing each day — that was new.

"Good girl." He let her go as promised. "Now come here and kiss me."

With perfect elegance, she turned around and climbed up over him, her whole body caressing his, his cock happily coming to the party, ready for round two, beyond ready to sink into the depths of her.

Soon...

She kissed him, a vulnerable tinge to her passion that pierced the hard, protective shell around his heart. And he gave in, allowing his emotions to flow through the safety of his actions.

Archer wasn't ready to express them out loud—might never be. He could hardly express them to himself, let alone commit his feelings to words.

Yes, he normally excelled at verbal expression—when things were easy and didn't challenge his status quo, his beliefs—but Temperance had him emotionally tongue-tied.

In keeping with their pact, he slowed the pace, softening the kisses to gentle, tender, affectionate, adoring. Cherishing. Because even if what they had couldn't last, she was special. The most special woman he'd ever met.

"You should officially move in." Something he'd never even considered asking anyone. And yes, it would help prove the validity of their union, back their swift marriage, but it ran deeper than that. He really liked hanging out with her, thoroughly enjoyed her company.

Living a bachelor lifestyle hadn't felt lonely, but since having Temperance around so often, the thought of returning to it was less and less appealing. However, he needed to keep reminding himself, he wasn't husband material. He wasn't a forever sort of guy. He favored variety, simplicity, freedom.

"I will...after we're married."

"Why not before? You're here most nights, anyway." Every night for the past couple of weeks, if he wanted to get technical.

"I don't know."

Oh, she knew...like he did. The more time in each other's space the higher the risk of obliterating the remaining boundaries and succumbing to overpowering primal needs. But he prided himself on his control. He'd stick to the designated parameters. And if he pushed too far, bordered on breaching a boundary, she only had to say 'stop' and he would.

"I'm not saying to give up your place. I just think being here will enhance our knowledge of each other and help support the strength of our bond. It'll make our decision to marry so quickly more believable. And going by how we've gotten on so far, it'll be far from a hardship."

A crease split the center of her forehead. "I suppose it makes sense."

So why did she look so uncertain, so unconvinced, so conflicted. "I swear I'll make it worth your while."

"Really? What does that entail? More sexual exploration?" She said it as though it were a negative.

"Did you enjoy popping your sixty-niner cherry?"

"I think my body already answered that question."

"Tell me with words."

She blew out a frustrated breath. "It was great, okay? Where are you going with this?"

Ah...so she didn't trust herself. "Confirming that you want the sexual exploration to continue, and it sounds like you do. So yes, that will be part of demonstrating you made the right decision to move in early. And there is so much more. You'll soon see how much I have to offer. How much fun we can have all around."

Her demeanor changed almost instantly, a sincere smile lighting up her stunning face. Obviously he'd said the magic word — something right — and appeased whatever remaining unspoken doubts had taken root in her head.

He pressed a soft kiss to her lips. "Let's get some sleep, and I'll help you pack up tomorrow. Consider me your personal removalist...with benefits."

Chapter Thirteen

The highly anticipated elopement day had arrived. A fortnight after Temperance had made the official move to live-in partners – the first time she'd cohabited with anyone outside of her immediate family.

A big step.

A massive step.

And for how long?

Such a pity it was a sham. Not their attraction, not her feelings for him, but how he viewed their future.

She stood in front of the en suite mirror and finished threading purple forget-me-not flowers into her hair. Her long, naturally wavy locks cascaded over her shoulders and down her back – the style Archer liked best, the style she'd captured in the painting she'd started.

She'd selected her favorite photo of them, taken at their engagement dinner, portraying their interconnectedness – their ecstatic smiles, their genuinely loving and affectionate gazes—through paint, mixed with her emotions.

The picture radiated pure joy, which seeped into her soul and transferred into her recreation on the canvas. The painting had taken on a life and energy of its own, as though the vibe had infused into the paint, into every brushstroke.

It flowed so easily she'd almost finished the candid portrait prior to them tying the knot. Her passion for the piece and super speedy vampire skills had helped. Once she'd learned a practical task, she could complete it in half the time of a full human, sometimes even quicker. But no matter how efficient she was, though, the paint still needed time to dry.

The image materialized in her mind, her photographic memory making every small detail come alive, filling her with exhilaration. Their upcoming wedding night might also have something to do with her elated state.

Given the primitive pull between them and their close proximity, she couldn't quite believe they'd been so principled, so disciplined, and refrained from having sex.

And now, with only a few hours to go until they were a legally married couple and alone on their honeymoon, she couldn't wait. Something more to inspire and invigorate her creative juices.

Upon returning from their ten days away to an undisclosed destination, she'd sneak in some time to do the finishing touches on the painting and give it to him as a surprise wedding gift. A memento of their time together.

She checked her phone screen. Not long until they had to leave. So, no more daydreaming…for now.

She'd reserve that for her spare, Archer-free time, not that she'd have much in the next few days. And she couldn't be more excited. Having him in reality way outweighed her imagination.

Although the marriage wasn't real in a you-complete-me, I-love-you-forever sense, it hadn't stopped her choosing a simple, white summery dress — beachy, bride-like, believable. It reflected her, no matter what.

She slipped on her something-blue garter, zipped up her new dress and secured the old, borrowed amethyst and jade earrings from her grandmother.

When Temperance had left for Australia, her *bestemor* had loaned her the antique jewelry as a way to make her promise to return to Norway. And yet now the heirloom earrings formed part of the plan to make her stay. Though, it didn't mean she wouldn't visit.

A gentle knock rattled the door. "Temperance, you nearly ready? The taxi's here. I'll load our bags and meet you out front."

"Okay." Nerves scurried in her stomach. Today was her wedding day, not at all how she'd pictured it. She'd dreamed of an intimate venue with close friends and family, all celebrating her nuptials, toasting to their new life together, she and her husband vowing to love each other eternally.

Maybe next time.

Though, she couldn't fault Archer. Since the inception of their rapid-fire romance, he'd held true to his word. He hadn't pushed for penetrative sex, though they'd tried almost every other sexual position and possibility.

And, as he'd promised, she'd had heaps of fun. Everything they did together ticked another pleasure box. *Time incredibly well spent.* She couldn't blame the man for embodying everything she desired in a partner. She was the one who'd gone off script and fallen in love.

Unshed tears burned the back of her eyes. She hadn't cried in so long, and now wasn't the time. She'd worry Archer, and she couldn't deal with him asking her probing questions. Couldn't answer them now, even if she wanted to, couldn't risk ruining her makeup, ruining everything…prematurely.

Temperance plastered a cheerful smile onto her face, grabbed her small white clutch bag and sheer shawl, slipped on her shoes, and joined Archer outside. He strode straight over, looking sharp, sophisticated and totally hot in a black linen suit, white shirt and black, violet and jade paisley tie.

He took her hand, his smile big, broad and appreciative. "You look" — he sighed — "breathtaking."

"And you look like husband material."

He laughed and kissed the back of her hand. "Come on, future wife. We've got a wedding to attend."

She took a step forward and stopped, a creepy vibe snaking up her spine. "Can you feel that?" She scanned the immediate environment, taking in every detail of the street and next-door neighbors' houses.

"Feel what?"

"Like someone's watching us."

"Who'd be watching? No one knows what we're up to…yet." Archer kept her arm linked with his, turned to her and held her face with his free hand.

"You're right. Must be wedding nerves or something." Except the crawling uneasy sensation didn't stop until they arrived at the registry office.

In no time, they saw the celebrant, said the required words, sealed their vows with the requisite kiss, signed the necessary paperwork with strangers as witnesses and were done — the production-line version of husband and wife.

But it did the job, made their partnership legal, official. They took some couple selfies, and Archer made sure the witnesses snapped plenty of pictures to add to their growing bank of evidence. Then he ushered her to their awaiting taxi.

An airport stop and two flights later, they landed at their honeymoon destination. Archer had organized it all, choosing a private, secluded island off the north Queensland coast, factoring in everything she loved — white sands, crystal-clear aqua water, rugged coastline.

Why? He could have chosen something simple, stereotypical, but still lovely, without going to this level of trouble and expense. She wanted to believe he strove to please her because he truly cared. But he was also strategic.

Had he selected an area she loved to ensure her reactions looked authentic, enamored, ecstatic when he took honeymoon photos, to possibly show to the visa assessors?

They picked up a rental car, and, after a short drive, arrived at the most amazing beach house she'd ever seen. So many windows overlooked a huge expanse of pristine seashore.

She wondered how the structure remained upright, secure, stable. She surveyed the surroundings and didn't see a single other residence or person in the vicinity. A true lovers' paradise.

While Archer dealt with their bags, she wandered into the kitchen. She searched through the fridge, pantry and cupboards to find them stocked with an abundance of food and drinks to cater to both their tastes.

A separate linen press had neatly stacked shelves filled with large, fluffy towels. They wouldn't need to leave their accommodation to stock up or have staff service the property during their stay. That, plus no TV, computer or phone reception equaled no unwelcome interruptions. Archer had covered everything.

Temperance entered the massive bedroom and stopped. Overhead, mirrors covered the ceiling, and mirrored inbuilt wardrobes ran right up to the glass. The unobstructed view stretched out across the expanse of white sand to the sparkling turquoise water, the waves rolling into the shore in a hypnotic rhythm.

To the right and left, rocky outcrops hugged the coastline, and wispy tendrils of cloud decorated the blue sky. *Paradise*. A week and a half of pure relaxation, and plenty of sex. *Absolute bliss.*

Archer appeared and wrapped his arms around her from behind. He'd discarded his jacket and tie, and had rolled up his shirtsleeves, his strong, sinewy forearms alone turning her on. He plastered his front to her back, his erection digging into her lower spine, demanding attention. "Nervous?"

About making love and viewing them doing it from every angle? *No.* About their arrangement ending in heartbreak? *Yes.* "Not with you. You make me feel comfortable."

"I hope I make you feel more than that." He swept her hair across her shoulder and nipped her earlobe. Her nipples hardened, and she let out a little moan.

Archer licked along the rim of her ear, and she sucked in a stilted breath. "Mmm…that's exactly what

I want to hear." He cupped her mound through her dress with one of his hands, and glided the other up to her breast and pinched her erect nipple. "Let me get you naked. I can't wait much longer to sink into you."

Her deliciously hot devil-of-a-husband never failed to get her juices flowing. Slowly, deliberately, he unzipped her bridal frock and peeled it off her body, leaving her in a matching white lace bra and panties, blue garter and strappy white shoes.

He turned her to face the mirrored wardrobe doors and sighed. "You really are exquisite." He unfastened her bra, his fingers warm, steady and agile, then crouched and slid off her lacy briefs and garter with his teeth.

Standing there nude, except for her high-heeled sandals, while he remained dressed, had desire pooling between her legs. He was right. She did love him taking control, exuding masculine power, in a sensual way.

Archer stood and watched her in their reflection, her core aching for his renewed touch. Her mind exploded with images of how he would take her their first time. How it would feel with him delving deep inside, their gazes locked, their bodies joined in the most intimate way possible.

Excitement surged through her. She would find out any moment now. He unbuttoned his shirt and stripped it off, along with his pants and boxers, adding to the growing pile of clothes on the polished wood floor.

"I'd love you to keep your shoes on and wrap your legs around me while I fuck you against the mirror but...next time. First, I'd like to commemorate our joining with something a bit more...in-depth."

"Such as?" Her breathy voice was barely a whisper.

"We spoke about doggy style with eye contact. So why don't we make the most of all these mirrors and give it a try? See whether you think it creates enough connection, if it lives up to all the hype."

She clenched her thighs together, her clit begging for some friction. "We definitely should test it out. It's important research to determine whether it's worth doing again."

His grin created devilish creases at the corners of his eyes. "Get on the bed, on all fours, and face the mirrors."

His commanding tone sent a thrill of anticipation through her already aroused body. She did as directed, and he climbed behind her. He palmed his cock and slid it along her drenched slit. She pushed back into him, silently requesting more rubbing, more pressure. More everything.

Archer leaned forward and feathered hot, moist kisses from the base of her head, all the way down her spine. "Dip your back."

He ran his warm palm over her sacrum as she adjusted her position. "Good girl. That's it." His words of appreciation and approval never failed to heat her blood.

Archer kneaded her butt cheeks, which unexpectedly lit up her libido. The man knew what he was doing, how to please a woman. Her. "Let me grab a condom."

Temperance met his gaze in the mirror. "No need. I'm on birth control, and I'm STI free." She didn't want any more barriers between them. She wanted their lovemaking to be free, spontaneous, special. Memorable. With unhindered full body, and, hopefully, emotional engagement.

"I'm tested regularly, and I'm all good, too." He lined up his cock, the head nudging her entrance, their eyes locking in their reflection. "Ready?"

"Ready and waiting."

She'd barely finished her sentence when he gripped her hips and eased his huge cock home, thoroughly filling her up. Slowly, deliciously, activating all her internal, super-sensitive nerve-endings. "Ohhh..."

Archer slid almost all the way out and thrust back in, over and over. "Fuck, you're so snug."

She closed her eyes and focused on the sensation of his dick sliding deep inside, hitting every single mind-blowing spot.

"Eyes on mine, baby. I want to see you're only thinking of me when you come on my cock."

As if she could consider any other man. Would even want to. No one had ever come close to Archer. No other guy had stamped their claim on her heart.

Temperance snapped her eyes open and met his desire-filled stare in the mirror. Watching them fuck, really did add another arousal-inducing dimension.

"Rub your clit."

Temperance hardly touched the super-sensitive little nub and pleasure spiked in her core. She whimpered and urged him deeper.

"That's right, baby. Take all of me." He picked up his fucking pace, thrusting forcefully, urgently, their skin slapping, the bed rocking. "I'm going to make you come so hard."

His words were a trigger, flipping her orgasm switch, and as he'd promised, the powerful pleasure reverberated through her in a full body climax. She screamed his name, bucking and thrashing, her core contracting repeatedly around his cock.

"Fuck me." He growled, stilled, his face contorting with the epitome of elation, and pumped his release inside her, like a man positively possessed.

He collapsed onto the mattress, pulling her with him, still buried deep, their skin hot and slick, delicious aftershocks pulsing in her pelvis.

Their recovering breaths and the crash of waves filled the room with a sexy yet soothing energy.

"So, what's the verdict?" He brushed distracting kisses along the corner of her jaw.

"You were right. It was amazing."

"It was. Best sex of my life."

Really? Wow. She hadn't expected him to admit that, even if it were true. It could cause complications, create a greater attachment…from her side. Exactly what he'd want to avoid. Though, their chemistry was undeniable. "For me, too."

"And how would you rate the connection?"

"High. Eight, maybe nine out of ten. Not quite as good as looking directly into your eyes, but close."

"I agree." He ghosted his hands over her breasts and stomach. "Next time…" He slipped out of her and rolled her beneath him. "You're going to lift your legs over my shoulders, and we'll stare into each other's eyes while I pound into you."

Oh God. Yes, please!

"We'll compare and contrast, and by the end of our honeymoon, see if our top five favorite positions correspond."

"Sounds like an excellent idea."

"Doesn't it? Days and days of enjoyment. Weeks."

Days, weeks. Not months. Because great sex didn't mean love. Looked like the duration of their marriage would rival the average high-profile celebrity. And yet, if she had to choose one word to sum up their relationship, it'd be *fun*. Fun, friendship discovery and earth-shattering sex, were their key themes.

He traced over her face with his finger, outlining her brow, her nose, her cheekbones, her jaw, her lips.

When he terminated their arrangement, how did he envisage they'd proceed? Had he thought about how they'd work together? Whether they could anymore?

Did he intend to remain friends? Had he considered the feasibility, the likelihood of sustaining some sort of successful casual involvement? Would he still want to hook up for sex? And if he asked, would she agree, while searching for her soulmate? Her brother certainly wouldn't approve. Not that he'd have to know...

"On the subject of enjoyment, we need some rules."

Her forehead puckered. "Rules? Rules and enjoyment don't exactly go together."

A mischievous twinkle flickered in his eyes. "You'd be surprised what goes together."

Come to think of it, overall, he wasn't wrong. Although attracted to him before entering into this scheme, she hadn't realized how well they'd get along. In every way. Had he?

Archer had spoken about their exceptional chemistry and compatibility, but were his words consciously or subconsciously hinting at the possibility of more? More interest. More longevity. More love.

"Enlighten me." She couldn't wait for him to explain how, in their current case, enjoyment and rules intersected.

"I propose no clothes. No inhibitions. No regrets. Total and utter honesty, openness and intimacy."

"For this afternoon?"

"No, for the entire trip. We're here alone—just us and the warm weather, the spectacular scenery, the amazing accommodation. So there is absolutely no good reason to hide…physically or emotionally."

She loved the idea of it but couldn't confide in him about the extent of her feelings. If she admitted she'd fallen for him, it'd make the rest of their time together incredibly awkward, and she'd hate that. While she had him, she wanted to maximize whatever opportunities arose.

His piercing gaze penetrated deep. "Are you in?"

Hopefully he would be again shortly. "Yes."

"Excellent." Instead of diving down for a kiss, he jumped up and rummaged through her suitcase, pulling out a tube of her special sunscreen. "Time for a skinny dip."

Archer slathered her with sun protection, grasped her hand and led her onto the beach. They ran across the hot sand and swam in the cool, soothing ocean, racing each other to some nearby rock pools.

Unsurprisingly, she won, and partway through her victory dance he emerged from beneath the sea right in front of her, a wicked gleam in his eyes. He cradled the back of her head with his hand, while he wound his other arm around her waist, and took her mouth in a slow, erotic kiss, the water lapping at their slippery wet, buoyant bodies.

Without warning, he threw her over his shoulder and powered through the water to reach a small expanse of sand in a secluded alcove.

The view was amazing. The scenery, a close second. Nothing could beat the man's magnificent butt.

She held tight to his hips, his arm across the back of her legs, his other hand on her ass and kept walking until they entered a cave. He lowered her onto her feet and spun her around so his front pressed to her back.

She sucked in a stunned breath. The natural architecture consisted of an intricate display of sparkling stalactites and stalagmites, surrounding and overhanging a blue-green pool. "Oh. It's stunning."

"You're stunning." He swept her mop of wet hair aside and kissed along her neck.

She shivered and angled her head to give him better access.

He glided his palm over her stomach and continued down, circling her clit.

She bucked into his hand.

He groaned. "I need to fuck you, baby. Right here. Right now."

"Yes!"

He steered her toward a smooth, waist-high section of rock. "Sit on the edge, lean back on your hands and spread your legs."

She carefully got into position, the surface cool and firm.

"Mmm...nice and wet." Archer stepped between her legs, gave his big erect cock a couple of pumps and thrust into her entrance. "Oh yeah. Perfect."

Her exact thoughts.

He fucked her quick and hard and desperate, and they both came in under a minute, the fastest she'd ever climaxed.

Once they recovered from their little impromptu interlude, they explored the cave and rock pools, holding hands the whole time, incorporating regular, super-erotic kissing stops, and returned to the beach house, where they made love in the shower.

They ate dinner on the deck, watched the spectacular gold, pink, purple and orange sunset and fell into bed, wrapped in each other's arms, their bodies intertwined, how they'd spent most of the day. A wonderful distraction, a fantastic escape from reality. Her own fantasy island. However, she couldn't avoid real life forever.

Archer lifted her leg over his waist, drawing her in so they fit tighter together, like a completed, three-dimensional puzzle. The way he held her felt so right, the closeness of their bodies exuding a synchronized energy, an aligned vibration that facilitated her to speak freely. To confide in him about her fears and concerns...everything except the full reality of her feelings. "When will we tell my brother?"

Up until now they'd avoided a lot of serious talk, too busy shoring up their scheme and doing each other. But they'd finally reached the pointy end of their phony relationship and needed, more than ever, to make their situation look convincing. Easy for her, because she wished all of it was real. But for him...

"About our horny-as-fuck honeymoon?"

"Be serious," she scolded. "He needs to know we're legally married ASAP. We need to give him time to get his head around it if we want him to accept and fully support us."

His validation was essential if they had any hope of achieving the outcomes they desired. Because, no doubt, someone from the immigration office would check the validity of her permanent visa application...and soon.

Archer angled her face until he stared into her eyes. "When we return, we'll give him a call, then tell everyone else. But while we're here, let's make the most of having no phone and social media reception. Let's make the most of *us*."

In idealistic terms, he'd made her dream come true. If only it could last.

Chapter Fourteen

Ten fucking brilliant days in paradise had come to an end. They exited the taxi and rolled their luggage inside his place. *Their* place, for the time being. Knowing he'd see Temperance every day, fall asleep with her at night, wake up to her in his bed, have endless opportunities to fuck, sounded extremely appealing...not restrictive. Surprisingly, he didn't feel even a hint of FOMO.

Maybe all the access to incredible sex had screwed with his rational mind. Now that they'd returned, would the brilliance continue? Their honeymoon, like their engagement and marriage, had exceeded his expectations.

Archer had always assumed he'd feel shackled committing to one woman. That matrimony would be like clamping him to a stereotypical ball and chain. A prisoner to a routine, monotonous, lackluster life.

Except he hadn't really committed, other than to their elaborate sham. So why did referring to their relationship as fake stab him in the heart with guilt and disgust?

Because, whether he wanted to admit it or not, she *was* different. They shared something special. But would their intense connection persist?

Still too early to tell. How much time together would convince him she was 'the one', as clichéd, cringe-worthy and saccharine as that sounded. Not that he believed in that shit.

He just needed to know whether their relationship had a strong chance of survival, longevity, without regret. But what marker would indicate whether they should stay a couple, even for a few months? What would determine whether they should continue together? Definitely not pressure. It had to be a joint decision.

One thing he knew for certain. He wanted to make a choice based off his own conclusions, not some soulmate serum, no matter how accurate.

"Archer?" Temperance touched his face, her spectacular eyes searching his. "You've been pretty quiet since we left the island. Is everything okay?"

He smiled at his bright, beautiful, perceptive wife. "Just adjusting back to normality."

"The new normal. It's not all bad." She trailed her fingers over his T-shirt-covered chest. "We can recreate and expand on some elements of our honeymoon. It doesn't have to end...yet."

He stilled her hand and held it over his heart. "I like your positive spin on the circumstances."

"Me, too. And, I have a surprise for you."

"Really?" He'd love to see how she could top walking around the house naked.

"Yes, but it requires you entertaining yourself while I go out for a few hours."

"Oh, I can entertain myself. Don't you worry about that. But my preference is to share the experience."

"Mine, too, but absence also has its benefits. It apparently makes the heart grow fonder."

"And my dick harder."

"That as well. Imagine how much passion that will add to our next sex session."

Mmm…welcome-home sex. "Expect me to pin you against the door the second you step back inside."

"I'd be disappointed if you didn't."

"Good girl." He patted her ass. "Now get yourself sorted and go so you can hurry up and return…before I ravage you and don't let you leave."

She twined her arms around his neck, pressing her bountiful breasts to his chest, and gave him a sweet seductive kiss, laced with promise. "See you later."

The moment she departed, his place felt empty. He missed her already. How fucking ridiculous. He sounded like a lovesick fool. Archer carried their bags into the bedroom, dumped them just inside the door, sighed and shoved his hand through his hair. Fuck, he had it so bad.

* * * *

Two afternoons in a row, Temperance had disappeared for several hours. What sort of surprise required that amount of separation? Archer normally didn't mind not knowing what his lust interest was up to, had no trouble keeping himself occupied, involved in his own agenda.

But with Temperance, it unsettled him, had him teetering on an unfamiliar edge. He needed her to keep him abreast of things, in the loop. Fuck, up until her he hadn't cared. He'd encouraged distance. Discouraged too much interconnected time, discouraged clinginess.

Never, in his long history of dating, had his mind diverted to all sorts of weird, worrisome and anxiety-provoking alternatives.

Instead of ruminating and driving himself down disturbing paths, he kept busy with housework, cleaning his car and cooking dinner—except he finished those tasks all too quickly.

He fidgeted and paced. If he didn't stop soon, he'd wear a channel into his floorboards, steamroll an uneven path through the carpet. What should he do? How did he usually keep himself occupied?

Workaholism.

Nope. Not resorting to that. He needed to sit with his discomfort, work through his avoidance and escapism, not give in to it, not attempt to slake his body's well-established addiction. Any emails requiring action would remain in his inbox until he checked them upon his return to work on Monday.

Archer dropped down onto the couch and scrolled through the plethora of pictures he'd taken of Temperance—of them—since they'd started on this unexpected, life-changing journey. So many fantastic shots, so many fantastic memories.

The front door lock clicked, and he jumped up, shoved his phone in his pocket and went to meet his wife.

He stepped into the empty corridor. "Temperance? Baby, where did you—?"

Someone grabbed him from behind in a headlock. Air squeezed from his lungs, his throat constricting like a squashed straw.

Archer elbowed the intruder in the stomach with all his force, but they didn't even flinch, their grip tightening.

"If you want to live, you better fucking listen. Understand?" A man's arctic, menacing voice practically formed icicles on his ear.

Archer hoped his stifled groan passed for a *yes*.

"You need to fuck your wife off and fire your business partner."

No fucking way.

"Nod if you understand."

He nodded, his vision turning blotchy. Didn't mean he'd comply.

The stranglehold eased up, and Archer gulped down mouthfuls of oxygen. "Why?"

"Because I said so." The intruder's icy cold breath froze Archer in place. "Maybe I should just get rid of the problem right now."

Two sharp points penetrated his skin.

A vampire.

Fuck.

Archer flailed his arms back but they hit vacant air. He tried to assess his surroundings, quickly determining the intruder had shifted to his side. He closed his eyes and, even though he was an atheist, he prayed.

Everything happened in an instant. The front door burst open, banging against the wall, and Temperance entered the foyer, holding a thin rectangular box. She gasped, dropped it, and ran toward him in slow motion, a loud crash sounding as wood smashed onto timber, jolting him into action.

He couldn't let anything happen to her. With every ounce of herculean strength, Archer shoved his closest elbow into the assailant's steel-hard stomach.

"*Ooof*," the guy groaned, caught off guard, briefly folding in two before he bolted.

Archer fell to the floor, relieved, and sucked down as much air as possible, worried he might pass out. Thank fuck she'd arrived when she had. Thank fuck the guy hadn't turned on her, because no way could he effectively defend his woman against someone with vampire genetics.

"Are you okay?" She dropped to her knees, running her hands over him as though to check for injuries.

He grasped her shaking hands. "I'm fine." *Now.*

"What happened?" Temperance searched his eyes, her tone frantic.

"I heard the door open, and I came to greet you, but got ambushed instead. Did you see what the attacker looked like?"

"Not clearly, but it was *him*. I'm sure of it."

"Him, who?"

"The vampire who immobilized that man after our engagement dinner. I know I didn't get a good look at the guy, but I'm certain it's the same person. His body shape and lightning-fast movement style matches. And although his eyes looked brown, he's definitely got vampire genetics."

"How can you tell?"

"The patchy, inconsistent shade of his irises suggested colored contact lenses. The plastic starts fading as soon as it mixes with vampire fluids. Add to that his presence, his hold on you, the venom in his voice…" She held his face. "What did he want?"

Archer hesitated. He preferred not to say anything, didn't want her to worry, but she needed to know the facts, the risks. "For me to break up with you and sever my business partnership with your brother."

"Why?"

"Exactly what I asked. I have no idea. Maybe some business competition? Someone who doesn't like mixed race relationships? Someone who wants you? Someone who wants me to fail?"

Her whole forehead crumpled with concern. "How did he get in?"

"Somehow he disarmed my house alarm system and came through the front door."

"We're not safe here. *You're* not safe here." Her voice quivered.

The logistic reality slammed him in the chest. He needed to come up with a solution and fast. Something that would reduce the danger without forcing them apart too early, because he wanted her, needed her right now. "We'll go to a hotel tonight, then I'll investigate the security issues and work on how to resolve them."

"How about my place?"

"If he knows where I live, chances are he knows where you live, too."

"Oh."

He wrapped her in a hug and stroked her lustrous long hair. "Let's get an overnight bag together and go check in somewhere with high-level security. Consider it an extension of our honeymoon."

She glanced up at him with a watery smile.

He held her face between his hands and peered into her wary, breathtaking eyes. "Everything will be fine." Or so he hoped. "Once we check in, I'll speak to my home security provider and try to determine how the guy overrode the system and what it'll take to prevent it from happening again. Then we'll call your brother and tell him our good news." Anything to keep her safe, to keep them both safe, and provide them with peace of mind.

The front door slammed shut, startling them both, his eyes darting toward the sound. No one there. *Thank fuck.* A part-splintered, part-shattered wooden box lay, like a cracked walnut shell, on the foyer floor, the corner of something poking out. "What were you carrying?"

Her eyes widened in horror, and she twisted out of his embrace. She jumped up and ran to the damaged box, delicately lifting and inspecting it, then opened the side and pulled out a canvas.

She scanned the picture, her eyes teary. "Thank goodness." She practically squished it.

What was so special about this painting? He stood and went to investigate.

"Stay there." She held up her hand in a stop motion, her eyes locking on his in a don't-you-even-think-about-taking-another-step stare.

"Does this have anything to do with my surprise?"

"Can you please go sit on the couch? I need a minute."

What the hell did it depict? Or had she bought him some collectible piece as a present? Either way, going by her reaction to the picture's possible destruction, it held significant meaning.

Although curious as all fuck, he did as she requested. Less than a minute later, she entered the living area looking a lot more composed, the front of the painting still facing her.

She held the canvas away from her heart, smiled, and met his impatient gaze. "Out of all the projects I've painted, I love this one the most. I often get into a state of flow when I paint, but this? It had an energy of its own. I've never completed something so quickly that captured exactly what I'd envisaged."

Temperance gently hugged the painting to her torso. "And yes, it is your surprise. I'd hoped to present it to you under very different circumstances but...we don't have control of everything. We don't have control of fate. I'm learning that more and more, with each day that passes." An almost sad, resigned smile seized her lips. "Anyway, I hope you love the picture as much as I do."

Her sweet, natural Temperance smile returned, tinged with anticipation, and she flipped the painting around.

Fuck. Wow. In mere minutes, he'd been struck in the chest, a second time, with overpowering emotion. The raw intricate beauty of what she'd produced, the accuracy, the way she'd encapsulated their essence... He couldn't stop staring at the canvas, at her. In his adult life, nothing had made him cry, but this... His eyes stung with threatening tears.

"Do you like it? Be honest." She studied him with a mix of hope and worry.

"No, I don't like it." He sprang up and strode over to Temperance, taking the painting out of her trembling hands and examining it up close.

"Oh."

His gaze flicked to her face, her eyes brimming with disappointment.

Shit. That hadn't come out right. He carefully reached around the canvas and caressed her jaw, angling her face until their gazes met. "Babe, I fucking love it. It's...beyond words. I can't even describe how incredibly amazing it is." His voice sounded hoarse, choked up.

A joyous spark returned to her eyes. "Really?"

"Yeah. I can't wait to put it on display. Make it the focal point of the room, take pride of our place. The second anyone steps in here, it'll draw their focus to it—to us. Capture our absolute positivity, as it does for me." He gently placed the picture on the living room floor, resting it against the wall in a tucked-away corner, and returned to his now-beaming wife.

She threw her arms around his waist and squeezed him in an affectionate hug. He could literally feel the love, relief and gratitude radiating from her body. "I'm so glad you're okay." Her soft voice shook with emotion.

Him, too. And so much more.

Their cue to leave. Archer held her equally tight and kissed the top of her head. "As soon as we get back, I'll mount your painting above the mantelpiece. But right now, we need to throw some stuff together and get out of here, so we both stay safe." At least in the interim.

Chapter Fifteen

After their scary, unsettling afternoon, Archer drove them to a swanky, high-security hotel in town, and they checked into the luxurious, golden penthouse suite. The sumptuous setting almost had her forgetting how close she'd come to losing her husband — prematurely. Permanently.

He plonked their overnight bag in the plush main bedroom and ran her a sensual, restorative spa bath, while he called his home security company. She hoped he could relay some reassuring news about how to reduce the risk of another potentially life-threatening attack.

Archer's voice drifted in from the next room, but with the spa jets on high, massaging the stress out of her muscles, she couldn't distinguish his words. She closed her eyes and focused on the rose, lavender and ylang-ylang scented water bubbling away and relaxing her body.

"Babe?"

She fluttered her eyes open to find Archer standing beside the spa, the soft, amber lighting enhancing the definition of his chest and abs and arms. Unfortunately, he still had his gray sweatpants on, though they did great things to highlight his incredibly appealing package.

He held out a full champagne flute and placed a small plate of exquisite handmade chocolates on the spa ledge next to her free hand. "You're looking significantly less tense than thirty minutes ago."

"The spa has helped heaps. Thanks for suggesting it." She took a sip of the pink champagne, and it tasted delicious—fresh, fruity, sparkly with a hint of sweetness. Usually she found alcohol tolerable at best, bordering on pleasant, but she drank it more to fit in than for the flavor. What did this drink have that differed from the rest?

"How is it?"

"Unbelievably good. Did you add anything special to it?" Like maybe a few drops of animal blood.

"No."

"Remind me to grab the name off the bottle and check the ingredients. Normally one glass of sparkling is more than enough, but I'd definitely have this again. It's oralgasm material."

"Wow. Nice. I'm so glad it hit the right spot. Not that it always makes a difference, but this is the top-end, expensive stuff—"

"That probably explains it." Or part of it. A little niggle inside suggested the overall explanation was something less simple.

"You've convinced me to grab myself a glass and join you," he said, and exited the en suite. Goodness, she loved that sinful sparkle in his eye. The insinuation, the silent promise of so much more.

He returned a couple of minutes later, gloriously nude, holding an empty glass and bottle of bubbly. "Top up?"

"Yes, please."

He filled her half-full glass almost to the brim, then poured some champagne into his flute and slipped into the water, opposite her, leaving the bottle within easy reach.

"You're right. This is good. Mmm…" He glanced at the untouched plate of chocolates. "Have one. I ordered them in specially."

For her. Which meant he'd factored in her vampire tastes and needs, pretty much admitting the recipe contained animal blood, not particularly palatable for human consumption. "How about you?"

"I've got my own small stash."

Even in a crisis, he'd considered both their needs. No wonder he'd done so well in a business sense. He'd shown he could think clearly, no matter the stress.

She took a bite of a dark chocolate ball with gold and blood red swirls. *Oh. Oh God.* She closed her eyes and moaned. The combination of ingredients came together to stimulate every single taste bud, while perfectly complementing the champagne. "Where did you get these? They're divine."

"I asked about food options, for both of us, and the concierge rattled off some cafes including a local boutique shop that sells vampire-friendly sweets. It got excellent reviews, so I figured it was worth trying. The concierge provided a menu, placed my order and arranged to have it sent up."

"Wow. Thank you. You've thought of everything."

A dark cloud of culpability descended over his face. "Not everything..." As in he hadn't been able to protect her during the scary situation earlier. He stared at her with single-minded assurance. "But I promise I'll get it sorted out."

"I know you will." She finished the chocolate and had another sip of sparkling, suddenly feeling a little floaty. Was this how it felt to get tipsy? Because if so, she totally understood the attraction. "So what did the security company have to say?"

"They'd look into it, review the software, hardware, check the camera footage. Try and piece together where the supposedly infallible system fell down."

The comprehensive approach was admirable, assuring, but sounded far from an easy fix. "How long will that take?"

"They're starting immediately and will keep me updated. No estimated time of completion yet."

Not surprising. "So, we could be here for days? Weeks?" Maybe even months. They could possibly live out the duration of their faux marriage right in this hotel.

"Possibly. Does it matter?" His tone fell into the concerned category. Not frustrated, not angry. Focused on her and her needs. *Such a considerate man.* Another reason to add to her growing list of why she loved him.

Did it disappoint her that they couldn't snuggle up and enjoy the comfort and coziness of his place? Absolutely. But ultimately, the only thing that mattered was their safety and being together.

When weighing up what counted, the destination didn't make a difference. "Not really. It's a slight inconvenience, but I'm sure we'll manage."

"We can do a clothes and toiletries run tomorrow, and I'll check if I can extend our booking here for a couple of weeks, initially. I'll let them know it could blow out further and see what options we have."

"What about work?" Should they risk making an in-person appearance or do their jobs from the safety of the hotel room?

"We'll return on Monday, as planned, and monitor things. I think it's important to show a sense of normality, to show whoever is behind this that we're not afraid. If there are any incidents or either of us feel unsafe, we'll re-evaluate. We can be adaptable. In the meantime, I've organized extra security to patrol the building and lifts, and to be stationed on our floor."

"Who's vetting the security workers? We want to make sure no one sneaks in or takes the place of an existing employee."

"I'll review all the applications and recorded interviews then have the final decision on who's hired. I'll thoroughly check all their credentials and ensure they physically meet their recorded anthropometric specs. Once hired, each time someone starts a shift and returns from any breaks, fingerprint and eye scanners will determine if they match their recorded information and identity."

"Sounds pretty foolproof." As long as the person hadn't found a way to override the safeguards...like they had with Archer's home.

"I hope so..." His voice trailed off, 'this time' not spoken but implied. Archer finished the rest of his drink and placed the flute next to the bottle. "Come over here."

She swilled the remainder of her sparkling wine, deposited her glass next to his and sat between his legs, her back to his front. She relaxed against him—the essential-oil-infused water lubricating their skin—and let out a contented sigh.

He kneaded her shoulders, a pleasurable sequence of sounds falling from her lips, her head lolling against his ripped chest. "How's that?"

Surrounded by Archer's big, hard body, she felt cocooned. Cozy. Safe. Loved. "Great. Mmm..."

"Don't get too comfy. We need to rinse off and ring your brother, remember?"

Damn. She'd hoped they'd fit in a bit of adult play first. Looked like she'd have to wait until afterward to indulge in some hands-on, adventurous Archer time. Hopefully the outcome of the call didn't spoil the mood.

She pulled the plug and swiveled onto her knees to face him. "Let's do this."

Archer grabbed her face and kissed her while the draining water whirled and sucked and whirred. Although the temperature in the room cooled, their intimate interplay kept her running hot...as always.

He tore his lips from hers, grabbed the handheld shower and adjusted the water temperature, thoroughly rinsing them off. They hurriedly dried themselves and dressed—unfortunately—sat on the couch and used her laptop to video call her brother.

Bror answered, the neutral expression on his unshaven face a facade, masking his feelings. She knew her brother. He could look as impartial as he liked, but a passionate mindset simmered below the surface. "To what do I owe the pleasure of this early morning wake-up call?"

Shit. She and Archer hadn't thought about the time difference. "Sorry! We have some exciting news and couldn't wait to share it." May as well jump right in.

Archer tightened his arm around her, an encouraging, you-can-do-this squeeze.

She glanced at her husband, his reassuring smile bolstering her confidence.

"So, are you going to tell me or keep me hanging?"

Temperance darted her eyes back to her brother, who'd lifted an impatient, I'm-waiting eyebrow. "Archer and I didn't just go on a holiday. We eloped." She didn't have to fake her joy, her enthusiasm.

"You *what*?" Her brother's cool mask had gone, replaced by shock and concern. "You only just started seeing each other."

"And things developed quickly." Archer looked at her like a man fully smitten. If only it were true. He loved the sex, they both did, but could he love her?

"No kidding." Bror shoved his fingers through his hair.

"Mate, I get that you're skeptical, given my history, but this is different. When you know, you know, and that's not dependent on time. It's about being open to and recognizing how you feel, the synergy, the sexual chemistry. Whether the relationship is practical, whether you share life goals, whether your partner is your best friend. And Temperance ticks all those boxes, and I tick hers, so here we are, husband and wife."

Her eyes teared up at his heartfelt words. He sounded so convincing. The sentiment had to have a thread of truth. Didn't it?

Lines of frustration slashed Bror's forehead, and he clenched his jaw, his lips a taut slit.

She inhaled a calming breath and stared her brother right in the eye. "I know it's not the path you envisaged for me, but I'm happy. Isn't that the main thing? Archer makes me happier than I believed possible. Can't you see that? Or is your ego too fragile, your biased opinion too rigid to admit your limitations, to view what's right in front of you?"

Archer stroked his hand in soothing circles on her lower back, exactly what she needed to stop her getting too emotional. Otherwise it'd work against gaining Bror's acceptance and support.

Her brother kept his eyes focused on hers. "You're not pregnant, are you?"

"What? No! It's not a shotgun wedding! Please, give us some credit." And yet the idea of having Archer's baby tugged on every single heartstring. Ridiculous, given they'd no longer be married in a few months, if they stayed on the current trajectory.

Archer used his successful businessman, no-nonsense stare on Bror. "We chose to wed. We weren't forced."

"At least that's one less complication." Relief replaced the frustration in her brother's face. "But I can't say I'm happy about your decision to get so serious so quickly. It's too impulsive. If you honestly believe you're so right for each other, why rush? Your working visa still has a bit of time left. Why not plan a proper wedding to reinforce the legitimacy of your feelings and desire to commit to one another in front of close friends and family?"

Her visa situation did have a bit more time to sort out, but Archer's inheritance eligibility didn't. Not that she could divulge that. She clamped her teeth together.

"What does 'proper' mean? Who's determining that definition? Neither of us wanted too much fuss—"

"Plus this was about us and our future, so we didn't see the value in dragging things out when we could officially be connected now." Archer really did always know what to say.

"We chose to spend the money we saved on a wedding on an amazing honeymoon instead." Memories of her and Archer making love while watching themselves in the mirrors, bombarded her brain. A rush of heat broke out on her chest and cheeks, and she coughed to cover up a moan.

"Spare me the details. Please." Bror's skin had a pinkish hue. "What's happened has happened, and I can't change it, so I have no choice but to accept the new reality."

Temperance sighed. Sometimes she forgot how staunch his stubborn streak could be, especially when he didn't get his way, if things diverted from the plan in his head. "You could sound a little more enthusiastic."

"I could, but then my answer would lack authenticity."

Stubborn *and* righteous. She barely refrained from rolling her eyes, even though he'd touched on, exposed, an element of truth.

"But I'll admit, you do look sincerely happy." His tone sounded surprised, like he'd assumed he'd catch them out during the course of the conversation.

"So does that mean you do support us?" She had to know where they stood.

"I'll always support you as a brother and Archer as a friend."

"How about us as a couple?"

"Do you need me to?"

"It would be nice." And helpful if the Immigration Department had further questions.

He scrubbed his still-sleepy face with his hands and exhaled a resigned breath. "I suppose it would be in all our best interests."

He didn't realize just how much...yet.

"Sorry for springing it on you, but we wanted you to be the first to know."

"I appreciate that."

"Any business updates while we've been on leave?" Clever of Archer to steer the subject away from them, now that they'd solidified her brother's acceptance.

Bror flicked his gaze to Temperance. "Remember your first boyfriend?"

What did he have to do with anything? "Beau?" The first guy she'd gotten serious about. The first guy she'd fully given herself to. The first time either of them had had sex. After that, he'd gotten a little too clingy and possessive, leading to the demise of their relationship.

"That's the one. He came to see me almost two weeks ago with a business proposition. Actually, more like a job offer."

"He tried to poach you?" Archer's what-the-fuck tone reverberated in the room.

"He wanted me to sever our partnership and partner with him in a rival company. I think he hoped for some financial backing from me, as well as my expertise."

Archer leaned forward. "I'm gathering you said *no*."

"I did."

"How did he take the rejection?"

"Not well."

Not a surprise. He hadn't taken hers well, either. For a few months after they'd broken up, she'd run into him at a range of places. Much broader than where they'd frequented when they'd dated. She'd almost suspected him of stalking. Then he'd started seeing someone new, and the weirdness had ceased.

"Did he threaten you?"

Why would Archer ask that?

"No. But he was very persistent, like he refused to take my 'no' as a permanent answer. He's sent me emails since, with some attractive offers, but nothing will entice me to change my mind. Especially now, seeing you're not only a good friend but also my brother-in-law."

Smart-ass. Exactly the sort of shit she'd had to put up with as a teenager. Sometimes even these days, particularly when he got into big-brother mode.

"Aww…you're the most considerate business partner a guy could ask for."

"I am, aren't I? Not to mention the best brother."

She couldn't stop an over-exaggerated eye roll. "That's the cue for us to let you go."

Archer peered into the laptop screen. "Keep us posted about this Beau character."

"Will do."

They ended the video call, and Archer angled himself so he could look her in the eye, his expression super serious. "Tell me about your ex."

"Why?" It shouldn't matter but somehow she felt exposed, like she'd done something wrong.

"Because my gut says he might be linked to the break-in."

"No. He wouldn't do something like that." *Would he?*

"Does he have vampire genetics?"

"He's a hybrid, but it wasn't him at your place. It's been a few years since I saw him, but I'd have recognized the guy." She'd known every detail of his face, every line, scar and beauty spot on his body. And as far as she knew, he didn't have any special powers that might affect his appearance.

"Doesn't mean he didn't arrange for someone to scare me, put me out of action."

Possible, but it seemed pretty extreme. "Just because he wants my brother to work with him and financially back his business?"

"And get you back."

What? No way! "That doesn't make sense. We split up ages ago and both moved on."

"You did, but maybe he didn't."

The bottom dropped out of her stomach. Archer had no idea how Beau had behaved in the past, and yet he made a strong, persuasive argument. Maybe her ex had appeared to move on, when he continued to hold a tireless, flaming torch for her and had just changed tactics. Maybe he'd gotten strategically smarter.

A cold shiver spiraled up her spine. "Should we say something to Bror?"

"Not yet. It's just a theory at the moment. A feeling. We've connected some possible dots but there's no real evidence."

"So what now?"

"Ensure we're well protected. Wait and see what Beau does next. Monitor him and his movements. Check if there are any pics of his affiliates online and see whether someone matches the description of our intruder."

"We should do that right now." The sooner they could prove or disprove Beau's involvement, the better.

She lifted her laptop onto her legs, brought up a browser, entered Beau's name and searched images. Lots of information about him and his new Norwegian company flooded the search engine, but none of the photos showed anyone who looked remotely like the guy who'd threatened Archer.

"Damn."

"Doesn't mean he's not connected to this. It was worth having a quick look to rule out any obvious association to him or his business, but I figured he'd be too smart to leave any easily detectable traces."

"It did say there were a few investors and a silent partner, and that Beau is considering expansion of the business internationally. So maybe one of those people is here. Maybe one of them is the man we're looking for?"

"Great pickup." Archer took the computer from her thighs, put it into hibernate and placed it on the coffee table. "Let's get some rest, and we'll investigate more tomorrow."

"Rest?"

"From this. Not from each other," he said, and pressed her back into the couch beneath him.

Chapter Sixteen

Alone in bed, Temperance rolled onto her side in an attempt to relieve the nausea and focused on the gains they'd made the last few weeks.

Within a month of intensive searching into Beau's business and with some help from a couple of Archer's security contacts, they'd tracked down pictures and names of the investors and discovered the identity of the silent partner, through a check of bank transfer records.

An image search online determined the guy in question lived in Melbourne and, from what Temperance could remember, looked identical to Archer's assailant. She and Archer immediately made a police report and, less than twenty-four hours later, the cops had taken the guy into custody.

He'd blabbed about his involvement in detail, leaving no doubt that Beau was the mastermind behind it all and had called the deadly shots.

And, unsurprisingly, Beau had gone missing, always two stealthy steps ahead. An unwanted, unneeded, additional stress. But would desperation make him screw up?

It usually set off a domino effect of poor decisions, leading to a person's demise or hopefully in this case, apprehension, preventing him from doing any further harm.

On the pretense of needing a sleep-in, Temperance had stayed in bed, waiting for Archer to be too busy to notice what she was up to. He'd gone to make breakfast and, thank the universe, his phone rang, and he answered straight away, his murmured one-sided conversation hard to decipher.

Questions circled in her mind. Where had her ex disappeared to? Had he escaped Norway and made it to Australia? Melbourne? Would he do something drastic? Personally put Archer's life at risk out of rising, reckless pressure?

She'd thought Beau had creepy aspects before but hadn't assessed him as dangerous…until now.

Temperance flipped onto her back and stared at the ceiling, as though hoping the answers would magically appear.

They didn't.

She had assisted as much as she could, in between waves of queasiness, human-food cravings and fatigue. Initially, she'd put it down to all the massive changes in her life, plus the Beau complication. But when the symptoms didn't subside, she did a Google search.

Pregnancy kept coming up as the most likely answer, except she couldn't have conceived. She'd consistently taken her birth control tablets. Hadn't missed a day, ever.

To rule it out as an option, she'd bought a couple of different companies' pregnancy tests. They'd hopefully provide a non-invasive, preliminary, conclusive second opinion. In the extremely unlikely event both tests came up positive, she'd book in to see a vampire-specialist gynecologist ASAP.

She stared at her sock drawer, where she'd stored them—a spot Archer wouldn't likely look—and impatiently waited for him to start pacing in the kitchen-living area, a sign he'd gotten so caught up in the call that he wouldn't notice her actions.

Compulsion to jump up and do the first test squeezed her stomach, but she forced herself to stay put, be certain he was preoccupied.

The moment Archer got into a striding rhythm and started discussing capture strategies, presumably with his security contacts, she covertly snatched the pregnancy tests from the drawer, ducked into the bathroom and locked the door.

With her heart thumping in her ears, she ripped open the first packet, her hands shaking so much she could hardly read the instructions, but somehow managed to successfully pee on the stick.

She set an alarm on her phone to bleep when the required time had elapsed. Minutes felt like hours while she waited for the test to process. She just hoped Archer wouldn't come looking for her in the meantime, question her about the locked door, about shutting him out.

Nervous knots twisted and tightened in Temperance's tummy, driving her to check and recheck the time, in case her phone alert didn't work. The alarm sounded, and her gaze darted to the indicator.

No!

The alarm kept going and going...

No way!

She snatched up her phone and shut off the persistent chime before it drew Archer's attention. The result couldn't be accurate. It had to be a false positive reading.

The edge of her vision blurred, the room suddenly spinning, and she stumbled, dropping the indicator in the sink and slamming her hands onto the vanity to stop from toppling to the tiled floor. She couldn't afford to faint right now, or the jig would well and truly be up.

Once steady-ish, Temperance grabbed a plastic bag from the cupboard, tied up the packaging and indicator and binned it. She ripped open the second test—a competing brand. Desperate and time-challenged, she somehow squeezed out enough urine to wet the test strip.

Again she waited, her gaze flicking between the elapsed minutes and the door. Finally the time came to check the result and...positive. Again. Part of her rejoiced, and part of her worried about his reaction. From the start, he'd clearly stated their relationship was a short-term arrangement. A baby made it long term, whether they remained a couple or not.

She'd assured him sex without condoms was safe. Would he question whether she'd led him on, gotten pregnant on purpose? Forced an outcome she desired? Hidden the truth? Flat-out lied to fulfill a forever-together fantasy?

He'd hate that. She would, too. Archer prided himself on honesty and expected it from others. If he thought she'd purposefully taken advantage, he'd never forgive her. How could she prove anything different? The circumstantial evidence looked damning.

Before she said anything to Archer, she'd have a consult with a hybrid-specialist gynecologist for absolute confirmation.

The door handle rattled, swiftly followed by a persistent knock. "Temperance, you okay?"

She swiveled her head toward the sound, her heart rate hammering. "Yes. Are you?"

"I'm fine. Why is the door locked?"

"Um…" No reason she could tell him…yet. "Hang on." She bundled up the newest test kit into another plastic bag and shoved it into the bin.

Temperance opened the door, and he stroked his knuckles along her cheek. "You look pale, baby. You sure you're all right?"

He probably thought her reaction was due to the Beau situation finally taking its tumultuous toll. Little did he know that possible added complications awaited them.

"Yes, given the circumstances."

He pulled her into a hug. "Good. I know it's been hard, much harder than anticipated. This was supposed to be a fun few hassle-free months for us. But I promise everything will get sorted. I promise I'll keep you safe."

His protector instincts had well and truly kicked in, which had the byproduct of dialing up her arousal. She clamped her thighs together. When didn't she want him?

Not the right time.

"I know." She didn't doubt he'd try his best to prevent her from further danger. But could his best protect him, protect her? Being one hundred percent human left him vulnerable, particularly from vampires.

"I missed you."

"I missed you, too. But, at the moment, the police finding and arresting Beau is the number one priority." On top of a possible baby.

"You're the best. You know that?"

"Yes, yes I do."

He laughed, squished her tighter, and kissed the top of her head. She wished she could bottle the blissful feeling, the joy and comfort of being held in his arms.

The hotel phone rang. "Let me see who it is, and I'll be right back." Archer raced out of the bathroom.

She entered the bedroom to find him sitting bolt upright on the bed, uttering one-word answers into the landline handset.

"Their ID checks out?" Silence, nods. "Uh-huh. Okay, fine." Archer hung up the phone, and she rushed over to him.

"Who was that?"

"Reception. Some worker from the immigration office has a few questions for us."

When it rained it flooded—or so it seemed since they'd returned from their honeymoon. Was it a sign from the universe? Was it a test to determine the true strength of their bond? How well they could weather the darkest of storms? Prove whether he was worthy of being the one?

She searched his eyes. "Are you worried?" Out of courtesy, Archer had informed immigration of their temporary address, but she'd hoped they'd process her application without an inquisition.

"No. We know each other well, and we have an insane amount of chemistry. It'll be impossible for her not to notice."

She hoped he was right, that it was as simple as he'd anticipated to pass her scrutiny, to tick the required permanent-visa boxes. But, more than likely, the assessor had a comprehensive battery of questions designed to highlight relationship red flags. They needed to prove their marriage had more than a physical foundation. That it had a significant spark, substance, sustainability.

People already tended to view the world through a skeptical, biased lens, let alone the Immigration Department. They'd have a directive to review applications with ultimate scrutiny. To find fault. Gaps. Inconsistencies in people's stories. Ensure the legitimacy of people's claims. Was that all their allocated immigration officer would focus on?

An abrupt knock announced the worker's arrival. Temperance rushed to answer the door, but Archer grasped her hand, stopping her a couple of meters away.

He leaned in, his sensuous lips close to her ear. "It's probably her, but always check the peephole, just to make sure." Archer kept hold of her hand and reached into the front pocket of his jeans to fish out his phone.

Using facial recognition, he unlocked the screen and opened a text message with a woman's picture and credentials. "Make sure she looks like this."

Temperance studied the woman's professional mug shot and committed her details to memory. Plus, she planned to ask her some questions to ensure her identity.

"Got it." She gave his hand a brief squeeze then walked the remaining distance to the door. She peered through the spyhole and observed the woman for a few seconds.

The worker looked like the picture Archer had shown her, and her eye color didn't appear doctored like a vampire contact-lens job. The woman stood still, her posture neutral, confident, almost relaxed, waiting patiently in a bright, floral summer frock. Not exactly the cheerful style she'd expected, but definitely not the sign of an impostor...so far.

"Can you please confirm your name and position?" Temperance continued to scrutinize the immigration officer, looking for the same types of troubling signs the woman would soon be searching for in her and Archer.

"Amelia, and I work for the Immigration Department, specializing in the assessment of permanent visa applications."

Temperance glanced at Archer to get his opinion, and he nodded as if to say, 'she passes. Let her inside'. She opened up and welcomed their visitor with what she hoped passed for a confident, relaxed, friendly smile.

Temperance introduced herself and gestured to her husband. "And this is Archer."

"Good to meet you." Amelia's smile looked sincere. *A positive start...or very strategic.* Maybe she intended to make them comfortable, at ease, lull them into a false sense of security and loosen their lips. Have them naturally offer up incriminating information.

He stepped forward, his most charming, charismatic smile in place and shook Amelia's hand. "How can we help you?" Archer gestured toward the living room settee.

Amelia sat on a single couch, and they took a seat on the sofa opposite. "I've reviewed your permanent visa application and have a few questions." She opened her red leather work satchel and took out a computer tablet.

The screen came to life, and she scrolled and scrolled down page after page. Were they *all* her questions?

She'd expected Ms. Sunshine to grill them somewhat, but not interrogate?

"Drink? Something hot, cold?" Archer asked, all Mr. Politeness.

Thank goodness one of them still had functional manners.

"Thank you. I'm fine for the moment." Amelia glanced up, smiled, then refocused on her notes. "This should be reasonably quick and painless. I just require some further clarification on a few things to ensure you meet all the criteria."

Archer subtly squeezed Temperance's hand. "What would you like to know? We're happy to answer anything."

They covered when they first met, when they realized they had feelings for each other, when they started dating, at what point they decided to take things further, when they realized they were a committed couple, what prompted them to take the next step and why so quickly.

They rehashed the answers they'd practiced and used with her brother. Amelia noted their responses, but her demeanor gave nothing away.

"Can you nominate someone who'd be willing to answer a few more questions to corroborate your story?"

"My brother, Bror, knows both of us well. I'm sure he'd be happy to speak to you." Temperance provided his contact details. "Anything else?"

"Not currently. Thanks for your time. I'll review all the information and feed back my recommendations. If I have any further queries, I'll be in touch. Otherwise, you'll hear from the department soon to let you know their final decision."

They all stood, and Archer shook Amelia's hand. "Great."

After they'd ushered the woman out and locked the door, he wrapped Temperance in a relieved clinch. "Close call. But I think we did well."

They had, but she wasn't worried about *their* responses. "Hopefully my brother won't let us down."

Chapter Seventeen

They carried on with life, working, living out of a suitcase, making love every night and morning, with no sign of their passion subsiding or Beau appearing. And although Temperance wished they could return home, somewhere more intimate, she understood the necessity of staying safe, first and absolutely foremost.

For Archer more than her. Though, his chivalrous side might disagree.

His home security company had identified the software and hardware breakdown — essentially the intruder had mimicked Archer's voice to perfection — but they'd supposedly resolved the issue by patching the software, introducing multi-factor authentication and replaced all the hardware with the most up-to-date, tried-and-thoroughly-tested, highly rated and reviewed products. Still, Archer insisted they remain at the hotel until Beau was found.

With more people around, plus beefed-up security and state-of-the-art cameras installed all over the hotel, including the lifts, it rated above his house as the safest place possible…if they stayed in Victoria. Otherwise, the next step would require them to move interstate or overseas. Hopefully they wouldn't have to resort to such extreme measures.

Temperance showered, dressed and drove to her specialist appointment, telling Archer it was a routine checkup so he wouldn't worry or ask too many difficult-to-answer questions.

Her symptoms hadn't abated, so she'd done another pregnancy test. And, unsurprisingly, it had also showed a positive result. Third time lucky or third time disaster? It all came down to Archer's response.

Actually, no, it didn't. If, worst-case scenario, he couldn't accept the circumstances, it wouldn't take away her joy about having his baby.

She parked without a problem, reported to the reception desk, and soon got called into her specialist's consulting room. Her nerves jangled like a wind chime in a blustery breeze.

"Tell me about why you're here today." The gynecologist smiled, her jade, violet-speckled eyes warm and encouraging.

Temperance sat forward in her seat, her hands fidgeting in her lap. "I think I might be pregnant but want confirmation."

"What symptoms have you experienced?"

"Fatigue and nausea mainly."

"Anything else?" The gynecologist's eyes searched hers.

"It's probably not related, but I've recently noticed more of an appreciation and craving for human foods."

"Actually, it's a common sign for pregnant hybrid vampires."

"Oh. Is it?" None of her half-blood friends had become pregnant to a full human, so she'd had no idea. Had no idea about what to expect, what specific nuances to consider, the parameters or timeframes.

"When did you start having sex?"

"About six weeks ago." She stared at her hands, more unsettled than ever. With each minute she spent in the specialist's office, the more it solidified the accuracy of the preliminary, unofficial results. "I've done three home pregnancy tests using different brands and each one has come back positive."

"Sounds like you have your answer."

"But I was on birth control, so I'd rather be absolutely certain before... I don't want to tell my husband if it's a false alarm."

The gynecologist leaned in, a concerned frown on her face. "Are you worried about his reaction?"

"Not worried exactly, but we only just got married. We haven't even spoken about family planning." *True and true.*

"I see." The specialist steepled her fingers and tapped them together. "Going by what you've told me, I recommend you start discussing children with him ASAP. Can you do that?"

As in, are you scared of him? Is he abusive?

That definitely wasn't the issue, but she appreciated the doctor checking. "I can. But it'll help if I have definite, unquestionable data."

The woman waved to the plinth running alongside the wall. "Then, please lie down so I can examine you and arrange for some further samples, some additional tests."

Temperance took off her shoes and got into a supine position, her heart about to beat right out of her chest.

The next do-or-die minutes could change the whole course of her destiny.

"I know it's hard, but try to relax. The more relaxed you are, the more accurate the reading." She wrapped a material cuff around Temperance's arm, above her elbow, and velcroed it closed. "I'm going to check your blood pressure and have a listen to your heart, then I'll do a skin pH swab. After that, I'd like a urine sample, and I'll have the practice nurse take some blood."

"How long until I know?"

The specialist gave her a reassuring smile. "We have a lab on-site, so you'll receive the results via text within the hour." She pressed the stethoscope to Temperance's chest, waited, made some notes, then took her blood pressure and pulse.

"Your heart rate's a little fast, but other than that, everything is within normal hybrid limits." The gynecologist grabbed a packet of swabs and four small clear containers from her desk and returned to the plinth.

She donned latex-free gloves, took out a thin white moist strip and ran it over Temperance's tongue, used another strip under her arm, one along the crease of her groin, and finally swiped the last strip across the lower part of her stomach. She stored one per vial and sat them on her desk. "They'll process within five minutes."

The gynecologist discarded her gloves in the closest bin, hand sanitized, and sent Temperance for a urine sample, then to have her blood taken, and afterward to return to the consulting room.

The clinic ran like a caring, efficient production line, and within half an hour she'd rejoined her specialist. Temperance stared at the containers on the desk and gasped. The strips had gone from pristine white to sparkling opalescent.

"It's nothing to be alarmed about. You're within safe levels. Let me explain." The woman held up one container. "Each strip indicates the presence of the hCG hormone produced by the placenta. So, in other words, you're healthy, and definitely pregnant."

Her knowledge and warm, gentle manner kept Temperance calm and on the verge of happy tears. "Oh. Um…great."

"The urine sample and blood results will confirm the specific hormone levels." She returned the bottle to its empty spot beside the others. "Given the data, if you haven't already, stop taking your birth control tablets."

Even though she hadn't been one hundred percent sure she'd conceived, she'd stopped the pill, just in case. The last thing she wanted was to potentially harm their baby. "I did, as soon as I had the first positive result."

"Good. I've seen many cases now where the fetus has overridden most forms of contraception and hasn't suffered any ill effects, but it's better not to take any chances." She reached into a drawer and pulled out a string of sleek, fancy condom packets.

"Regarding long-term family planning, I'd recommend using these — sun-infused condoms. They are ninety-nine percent guaranteed to prevent your vampire genetics from eating away the protective rubber. In my experience they're significantly more successful than the pill and regular condoms in terms of preventing pregnancy. They're more expensive, but they're worth it."

She slotted them into a small, discreet bag and handed them to Temperance. "If you're happy with the samples and would like to buy more, you can purchase them through this clinic or via vampire-friendly pharmacists."

"Thank you so much." Temperance tucked them away in her handbag.

"Let's book you in for a scan in two weeks to check how the baby's progressing and determine a due date."

Temperance left the office, her mind spinning with a barrage of thoughts and scenarios, and an overabundance of feelings. She reached the car, dropped into the driver's seat and touched her tummy. In a few short months, she'd become a mother.

A beaming, impossible-to-tame smile overtook her face. She couldn't quite believe what fate had delivered. Things didn't always go to plan, but that's because sometimes the universe had bigger, more exciting ideas in store. Right?

Knowing she carried Archer's child filled her with an overflowing fountain of joy. But how would he take the news? And when should she tell him?

* * * *

Archer paced the hotel room. Temperance had left ages ago and, with Beau still on the loose, he couldn't help but worry. "I should have gone with her," he mumbled, and thumped the wall with his fist. "Stupid. Fucking stupid." He shoved the heels of both hands into his eye sockets and tried not to panic.

A loud slam had him dashing to the front door.

Not Temperance.

Beau.

Fuck.

His heart rate took off like an Olympic sprinter.

The on-the-run hybrid stalked toward him without a care, oozing confidence, a snide smile on his face. Soon the guy would have him pinned against a wall with no escape.

Archer surveyed the room as subtly as possible, without taking his eyes off the scary-as-fuck fugitive, his pulse pounding in his ears. With only one exit — currently blocked by Beau — he could try to barricade himself...somewhere. But how long would he remain safe? The guy could break down the door or through a plastered wall in seconds.

Or, if luck had really deserted him, Beau could also have special powers. For all Archer knew, the guy could fucking walk through walls or turn back time. Or possess any number of skills that defied human ability.

Fuck. Fuck. Fuck.

Hopefully he hadn't gotten to Temperance first. Not that Archer could do anything about that now. He had to focus on how to survive or he'd have zero chance of seeing her again.

The hotel phone rang, the persistent ringtone blaring in the silence.

The phone.

Yes.

He had to find a way to make a call to security. Either that or die.

"Don't answer." Beau's ice-edged voice assaulted his spine like a snowstorm, making him shudder.

"How did you get in here?" Archer backed away, but Beau continued forward.

A sinister smile split the evil prick's lips. "Let's just say I created a little diversion requiring the assistance of security staff on every floor to address the potential threat."

Each menacing step drew him closer, leaving Archer fewer and fewer options to get away. "So it looks like it's just you and me, unless Temperance is hiding somewhere? Temperance, baby? Come and say *hi*," Beau called out, a smart-ass smile on his face. He cupped his hand behind his ear as though listening for a reply. After a few seconds he stopped and threw his arms out wide. "Apparently we're all alone up here."

Thank fuck Beau hadn't found his wife first.

Whatever distraction the guy had created couldn't have been too little either, if it had required every security staff member to leave their post.

Archer fumbled in his pants pocket for his mobile, pressure, desperation and the stubborn desire to live driving him to push on, no matter how low the odds of his survival.

"I'll take that."

Before he could register what had happened, Beau had snatched his phone and thrown it with such force that it smashed against the floor.

Fuck. Archer struggled to breathe, the guy's palpable aggression clogging the air.

Beau crowded into his space. "Where is she?"

"Out."

He slammed Archer up against the wall, Beau's forearm crushing his airway. "When is she due back?"

Archer couldn't answer, even if wanted to, which he didn't. He didn't want to put Temperance or himself at greater risk. Not that things could currently get much worse for him.

He coughed and wheezed, struggling for oxygen, black splotches hampering his vision.

"If only you'd have come onboard." Beau shook his head, his eyebrows pulling together with faux concern.

"If only you hadn't crossed me, I might have saved you."

As if. Whether Archer had played nice or not, he was an unwanted loose end, a threat. Someone who needed to be eliminated.

Beau released his death grip and lunged forward, biting Archer's neck.

His knees wobbled, buckled and he collapsed onto Beau's body. The man didn't budge. Not a millimeter. However, his scalpel-sharp teeth did, sinking in deeper.

Contrary to what Archer had thought, it didn't feel unpleasant. The double puncture into his skin plus the sucking created a trippy, drugging fog. Not the worst way to die.

"Archer?" Temperance's sweet voice traveled straight to his heart.

No! 'Run' died in his throat, his powerless voice petering out. He couldn't protect her.

Her hurried footsteps approached. "There was some commotion downstairs. Are you...? Get away from him!"

Halfway gone, less than half aware, he crumpled to the carpet. A blurred, muffled fight broke out before him, and he tried to stay conscious.

His fierce woman battled with Beau, sinking a couple of haymaker punches to his face, kneeing him in the balls and wrenching the guy's arms behind his back, seeking a hard-fought reckoning. He thrashed and struggled, but before he could retaliate, she pressed a spot in his neck, rendering him unconscious.

Beau dropped to the floor with a thud.

Out cold.

The element of surprise plus her determination and level-headed strategic approach had come together and overpowered the guy, putting him out of action. Growing up with an older brother and having to defend herself during sibling scuffles had probably helped her learn a few moves too. *Fucking impressive.*

She rang hotel security, then the police, and dropped to her knees beside him. "Archer, are you okay?" Temperance touched his face and continued speaking before he could utter a word. "You know what? Whether you say you are or you're not, I'm calling an ambulance. Just in case."

If he'd been turned, he needed quick access to the vampire anti-venom.

She phoned the paramedics, explained the circumstances and requested they bring some vials of the vampire-bite antidote, then wrapped Archer in a tight, affectionate hug.

Less than a few minutes later, security staff entered the room, closely followed by the police. They restrained a still-unconscious Beau's wrists with sun-infused handcuffs and took him to the station for questioning. Well, they'd throw him in a holding cell first, unable to interrogate him until he came to.

The ambulance arrived, checked Archer over and administered the vampire anti-venom as a precaution. Other than that, they gave his general health a gold-star rating, recommended he contact his doctor if he developed any concerning symptoms and departed.

One of the plain-clothed policemen approached them soon after, took their statements and finally left, along with his staff, who'd gone through the penthouse with a finer-than-fine-tooth comb, collecting evidence.

Alone with his woman had never felt so good. He kissed Temperance with relief and gratitude, and they fell into bed. Facing each other, they made love, the most intimate connection he'd ever experienced.

She stared into his eyes, hers still sparkling with an orgasmic afterglow. "I love you."

Commitment alarm bells went off in his head, activating all his barricades. He stiffened. Too soon. He wasn't ready, might never be. Hence why they weren't meant to develop feelings for each other, get attached beyond lust. It complicated everything. Their arrangement was meant to be fun with no strings and a mutually satisfying outcome.

So why did his heart like her saying those three scary words?

Fuck, fuck, fuck!

"Archer?" The vulnerability in her eyes almost slayed him, cut him deep to his emotionally compromised core.

"We should get some sleep. A lot of exhausting shit has happened." And he needed time to work through his mind-versus-heart conflict.

Chapter Eighteen

The next day they returned home — well, to Archer's house — but he still acted all weird and distant. Telling him 'I love you' had felt right last night, and yet he'd reacted badly. Worse than Temperance had imagined, and he still hadn't recovered.

Given the gravity of what had happened with Beau, how close Archer had come to death, she'd believed it'd draw her and, well, her faux husband closer...not push them further apart.

The issue with assumptions — they linked to a person's individual way of thinking rather than factoring in differences, considering the breadth of the situation. Just because the events had deepened her feelings for him, didn't mean they had impacted on Archer in the same way, as evidenced from the moment she'd gotten all gushy.

Archer disappeared into the main bedroom with their bags. Although he'd hardly said two words to her since she'd laid herself emotionally bare, he'd remained civil, pleasant, courteous. He'd descended into avoidance, and she didn't know how to bait her line to hook him back in.

Even if she did manage to reel Archer in again, depending on his mindset, she might still have to let him go.

He emerged half an hour later and entered the kitchen. "I've unpacked everything and put a load of washing on."

How very domestic…and superficial. How escapist. But she couldn't force him to engage in a deep and meaningful conversation. He needed to instigate that. "Thanks."

"Want a coffee?"

She'd prefer something alcoholic, but since her pregnancy diagnosis, she had to avoid the stuff. Considering how he'd reacted to 'I love you', thank goodness she hadn't blurted out the baby news. He'd have gone into meltdown.

However, assuming she didn't miscarry, she'd have to tell him…eventually—once she hit the safe, three-month mark. By then she'd have a better picture of what her future looked like and how to best announce he was going to be a father.

In the meantime, she'd give him a bit of grace, some leeway to express his feelings and confirm whether he'd uphold his initial stance to remain an eternal bachelor—or if he'd choose her. "No, thanks. I'll grab a soda water."

"I'll get it."

She sat on the couch, where they'd made out so many wonderful times, leaving a spot for him beside her.

He carried his coffee, and handed her the soda water then sat opposite, crushing her heart, pulverizing it into tiny broken pieces. His reluctance to sit next to her silently said so much. Up until her admission, he couldn't keep his hands off her, and now, it was as though he couldn't stay far enough away.

All his hurtful micro-behaviors struck at the same wounded spot, leaving it sore and open and bleeding. Each time he pulled back it left a larger hole, adding to the damage of her pre-existing scars. She gulped down her drink, anything to stop her bursting into tears.

He sipped his coffee and struggled to look at her. "I won't be at work for the rest of this week. I've got a conference in the city. It's a great networking opportunity, so I've arranged to stay in town."

Since when? He couldn't wait to return to his home, and now that he had, he couldn't wait to run away. When would he realize he couldn't escape discomfort forever?

Not yet. Not while he continued to trawl the internet to find something, anything, to reduce their time together.

She stifled a sigh. "Oh. Okay." Not really. Far from okay. However, she had no choice. She wanted a resolution but had no control over his behavior, or whether he was in a headspace to listen.

If only she could call her brother and offload all her emotional baggage. But she'd been complicit in the charade and so had to take responsibility. She had no right to complain that Archer didn't reciprocate. He'd never promised her love.

Did she want to remain in a relationship that couldn't offer her that?

No. But she refused to use the baby as leverage — emotional blackmail. She wanted her partner to love her equally, of his own volition, not because she'd given him an ultimatum and tried to strong-arm the outcome she desired.

Archer sculled the rest of his coffee and stood. "I need to get on top of some work requests, seeing I won't be available for the next few days."

He rinsed his cup, disappeared into his office and shut the door. The rest of the afternoon, he remained confined to his man cave, while she did her own thing. She'd give him until Friday. And if he didn't snap out of his funk, his silent-treatment status, she'd need to seriously reconsider her options.

She loved him, more than any man she'd ever met, but she couldn't hold out indefinitely, hoping he'd change his mind, change his long-term mission regarding relationships and come onboard. Setting up expectations would only lead to further disappointment.

She had to go with the facts and weigh them against what she wanted. If either partner had to overcompensate to please the other, as a couple, they would never work. The opposite. They'd be doomed.

Temperance didn't want that for herself or her unborn child. Ultimately, she required a man who loved her and her offspring, so if Archer couldn't offer that, she needed to find a guy who would.

Unable to concentrate on any one task for too long, she turned her attention to making dinner, a choice influenced by her unborn baby. Temperance craved a home-made shepherd's pie in a ramekin without pastry — a minced meat mixture topped with mashed potatoes and accompanied by baked veggies.

Within ninety minutes, their evening meal was ready. She knocked on Archer's office door, eased it open and let him know.

"I'll be there in five," he said without lifting his head, his hair a ruffled mess.

Within the timeframe he'd specified, he joined her at the dinner table and dug into his food, offering superficial, detached conversation, focusing primarily on how much he enjoyed what she'd prepared. Afterward, he thanked her for cooking and washed up, then retreated to his safe space. His don't-bother-me den. His Temperance-free zone.

She waited up for him, but it got to eleven p.m., and she could hardly keep her eyes from sliding shut. Prior to the pregnancy she'd had more energy, but now, fatigue overwhelmed her like a sleep spell. Archer's lack of interaction didn't help, either.

And because he had entrenched himself in avoidance mode, he hadn't even noticed the changes. Probably a positive. She didn't want any of his decisions made out of a sense of obligation.

Half asleep and majorly disappointed, she slipped into bed and woke up the next morning without knowing whether he'd joined her. She yawned and stretched, his side of the bed cool to the touch, and his packed overnight bag gone, right along with him.

Each night after he'd left for the conference, she frequently glanced at her phone, hoping he'd call, message, something. Communicate in some way. However, outside of an SMS to let her know he'd arrived safely and that the inheritance from his great-uncle Salvator had been approved, she'd heard nothing.

No further texts, DMs, emails, or voicemail messages.

It got to Friday, and his silence had fortified her decision. An unwanted decision, but a necessary one for her mental health and wellbeing, as well as their baby's. If he didn't love her, she didn't care about the visa.

Not now. Initially she'd wanted to stay in Australia for so many reasons, but none of them seemed relevant anymore. With a little one on the way, she needed reliable support, caring and love.

Temperance sat on the couch and opened up her laptop, searching for flights back to Norway. She hovered the cursor over a one-way plane ticket, an internal debate warring in her head. Should she stay whether they were together or not, so her child could know, and spend time with, their father?

Or should she do what would best support her now and rethink options later?

She went to buy the ticket and stopped, the mounting tears in her eyes blurring her view. She wished she didn't have to leave but didn't want to outstay her welcome.

Temperance swiped at her eyes with the back of her hand. The screen darkened, ready to go into sleep, and she clicked.

A purchase confirmation filled the screen, noting that a copy would be sent to her email. It pinged seconds later.

Done.

No going back.

Best for both of them — the three of them.

Somehow she packed without breaking down into a tearful mess, and left Archer a note with her resignation and an explanation of why she'd chosen to return to Norway. With nothing further to lose, she poured out every inch of her heart.

The taxi arrived soon after she placed the folded-up pieces of paper, with Archer's name scrawled across the top, on the dining table. With no more time and her feelings scraped-to-the-bone raw, she grabbed her suitcase, passing her painting, which Archer had promised to mount above the fireplace.

And hadn't.

She wiped away a tear trickling down her cheek and said one last goodbye to what she'd started to believe was home.

* * * *

Archer arrived at his place late Friday evening and checked the mailbox. He reached in and grabbed a bunch of letters, unable to delay entering his house any longer. How would Temperance respond to him? He'd given her radio silence all week. Guilt festered inside his gut like fetid, rotten fish.

A couple of deep breaths later, he stepped through the front door, the space unnervingly quiet, devoid of her palpable presence. Empty. Maybe she'd gone out? Gone to after-work drinks with some of her colleagues?

"Temperance?"

No answer.

He did a quick walk-through and...no sign of her. Served him right. He'd acted like an immature prick, the exact fucking loser her brother had warned her about. Did he really want to be that guy anymore? Scared to commit in case he made a mistake and failed?

If he carried through that mentality in the business world, he'd be fucked. It was no way to live.

He dropped his bag in the bedroom and sifted through the mail in a distracted daze. An official-looking envelope stood out. Did it hold the answer he and Temperance had hoped for regarding her visa?

Archer ripped open the letter, and speed-read through the contents, confirming she'd met the permanent visa criteria. What a fucking fantastic welcome home. He'd met his great-uncle's will specifications earlier in the week, and now she'd been approved to stay in the country. The result had absolutely exceeded his expectations.

But even more important than sharing the news with her, he needed to apologize for being such a dick...then maybe have some makeup sex.

Archer went to leave the letters on the dining table and a folded-up note with his name in her handwriting glared up at him. *What the fuck?* She'd have text messaged to let him know where she was, not leave some massive missive. Unless...

His heart rate took off like he was running for his life, curious, yet frightened, to read what she'd written.

With trembling hands, he tentatively unfolded the paper and read her beautifully elegant script, dated today.

Dear Archer,

You're receiving this because I can't do the fake thing anymore. When I told you I loved you, I meant it. You are so much more to me than a means to an end. I wanted to remain detached. I didn't intend to develop real feelings, but I did. Your behavior told me you didn't.

It made me realize I couldn't continue with the charade. If you don't love me, why would I stay? I don't care about the permanent visa if I have to live here without you as my partner.

I can't go back to being friends and forget about what we shared. I can't keep seeing you every day at work, knowing we're over, that I can't come home to you. I thought maybe I could, but it's too torturous to have you so near, yet so emotionally far.

Please find my resignation letter enclosed. I have returned to Norway to start afresh. I will always cherish our time together. You're the first man I've ever truly loved, and a piece of my heart will belong to you forever.

I wish you every happiness.

Love always,

Temperance.

"No!" he shouted and slammed his fist on the table. What had he fucking done? Driven her away with his stupidity.

He thumped his palms onto his forehead and dragged them down over his face, his jaw tight, fighting back fear. He had to fix this. Had to get her back. Tell her, show her he cared. No, not just cared.

Archer had never thought he'd fall for anyone, but he fucking loved her with every inch of his heart, his mind, his body. He couldn't do casual anymore. She was the one and only woman for him. He didn't need to take any soulmate serum to convince him of that fact.

His gaze fell to the picture she'd painted of them. So happy, so in love, even though he hadn't recognized what was right in front of his face. Until she made the ramifications very real, life-changing—and not in the way he wanted.

He couldn't lose her. Not now, not ever.

Wallet, *check,* mobile, *check.* Keys in hand, he jumped into his car and floored it to the airport. He had to find her, stop her from leaving. Bring her home to him. Permanently. Because he fucking loved her beyond words.

Archer entered the multi-level parking lot, threw his car into a spot near the international departures section, and ran inside, a man on a recovery mission.

He scanned the flights board, searching for the next plane to Norway, praying she hadn't caught an earlier one.

He needed to stop her from boarding, if she hadn't already. But how?

Think. Fucking think.

He couldn't afford a moment's hesitation. She'd take her seat on the aircraft, and he'd lose her. He couldn't fucking do that. Not since he'd found her. Found himself.

Excited travelers rushed by him. He shoved his hands through his hair. *Come on, come on!*

A boarding gate announcement came over the speaker.

A boarding gate announcement?

She'd have to take notice of that. He located the check-in desk, spoke to a staff member, who had a full set of romantic bones in his body, and requested a huge favor. In between the list of boarding gate information, his message, *Temperance, I love you. Will you marry me, for real?,* flashed up in bold, bright lights.

The staff member followed up the visual announcement with a voice broadcast, requesting Temperance to report to the boarding gate counter.

"Come with me," the man said with a twinkle in his eye, and he accompanied him to the relevant departure lounge.

Before Archer saw her, he felt her presence, as always.

Their eyes met, almost instantly, her face happy, exuberant. She left her luggage at the counter, broke through the crowd of eager travelers and launched herself into his arms. "You came?"

"Not in the way that I'd like, but we can organize that afterward."

She laughed, and it was the sweetest fucking sound. Temperance touched his face, her expression morphing into serious mode. "I love you, too, and yes, I want to be your wife for real. But first, there's something I need to tell you, something you need to know."

"Are you okay?"

"Mostly."

"Mostly?" He swept her hair off her face and searched her eyes.

"I'm pregnant."

"Pregnant?" *Fuck*. He'd suddenly gone from husband to expectant father. A fucking massive shock. But all that had stemmed from the most enjoyable three months of his life. Who could ask for anything better?

"Remember—"

"You don't need to explain." And he meant it. Was he stunned? Fuck, yes. Happy? One-hundred-fucking percent.

A huge smile split his face. "I'm excited. Beyond excited. To have you back, to have a baby on the way...with you. Best fucking day!" The opposite of what he'd ever believed he'd say, if confronted with the news he had a partner carrying his kid.

"For me, too. But what about my visa?"

"Granted."

"What?"

"The letter arrived today."

"We really are meant to be." She stared at him with so much love.

He squeezed her tighter and kissed her lips. "We are. Now let's go home and celebrate."

Want to see more from this author? Here's a taster for you to enjoy!

Hearts in Danger: Sage Advice
Sandra Carmel

Excerpt

"Visit Alexander? No way. No. Way. He was an arrogant prick to me back in the day." Sage Cassidy shook her head, adamant, and refocused on her laptop screen. And yes, okay, she might still harbor some slight, unresolved feelings following his rejection.

"Prick? That's a bit harsh. I know he can be stand-offish." Chase stared at her with his over-observant lawyerly eyes. "Did he do something you didn't tell me about?"

Where did she start? She raised her eyebrows in a challenge her brother couldn't win. Chase had blind loyalty to his best mate. He couldn't refute her, unless he knew something she didn't.

Which was entirely possible, considering she hadn't communicated with, let alone seen Alexander Barrett in fifteen years. "You mean, other than him treating me like crap since I turned twelve—teasing or ignoring me, then essentially ordering me to fuck off when I tried to hang out with you guys?"

Chase sat forward and propped his forearms on his knees. "Okay, fine. I get that he can be gruff, but he has a good heart."

Ironically, Alexander's gruffness turned her on, the idea of trying to win his affections…except he'd looked at her like she represented some defective female alien from another planet.

Sadly not surprising given she'd been a gawky rather than pretty teenager. So, massive fail. Her crush's supposed *good heart* left long-lasting effects.

Not that he'd have any inkling about the impact he'd had on her love life, men, relationships. As a psychologist, working in the trauma field in Melbourne for years, she should really talk about her unresolved feelings in her supervision sessions but…avoidance continued to be her favorite coping—more accurately, *non-coping*—strategy. "I can't see him. Sorry."

"Sis, please…for me. He's had a really rough time. He can't return to the military, and he's feeling lost, useless, helpless, when he's used to fighting for his country. Being the tough guy. Invincible." Chase focused his imploring eyes on her, his fingers fiddling with his platinum and sapphire cufflinks, the ones their now-deceased parents had given him as a graduation present.

How could she say no to that? She knew all about military-induced post-traumatic stress disorder. She'd specialized in it, worked with ex-service staff every day using eye movement desensitization and reprocessing—EMDR—therapy, combined with counseling. It constituted her bread and consistently warm, melting butter…when her intervention worked. And it didn't always.

"Did you explain you'd be asking *me* to make contact?"

"Yeah." He tugged at the sleeves of his expensive, immaculately pressed navy suit. Between that and the crisp white shirt, he looked fresh, like he'd just gotten dressed. He hadn't, though. He'd been in court all morning. 'Workaholic' had become his middle name — dependable brother, workaholic, best friend.

"And he was fine with it?" She couldn't believe Alexander had agreed.

"Totally. He refuses to speak to a stranger. He even refused to talk to me!" Chase slammed his hand to his chest. "That's when I realized things were serious. I tried to get him to open up for hours and…nothing. He said he didn't want to burden me, that what he'd seen had changed him permanently and the one steady thing was our friendship — something he didn't want to jeopardize. I get that. Well, maybe not 'get it' exactly, but I can empathize."

Chase adjusted his paisley tie. She'd never seen her brother so rattled. Normally he radiated confidence bordering on cockiness.

Sage nodded. She sensed he still had more to offload, more to say to attempt to get her onboard. And he excelled at arguing, debating.

"I convinced him to speak to someone, and he agreed, under one condition. It had to be a person he felt comfortable with, but no one too close. I thought of you straight away. Plus, given your specialty…"

Disappointment stabbed at her heart. *Bloody, unresolved emotional crap.* It wasn't like Alexander had ever shown a hint of interest in her romantically, even though she'd wished he'd finally *see* her — the *real* her, her as a grown, self-assured, desirable woman, not Chase's awkward, bothersome sister.

Instead, he'd demonstrated the exact opposite — except that one night when they nearly kissed, right before he left for the military…after his farewell bonfire. They were alone, and she ran her hand over his newly close-shaved hair, assuring him he looked cool, tough, mean, and no one would want to mess with him.

He'd grabbed her wrist, the flames of lust in his eyes practically melting her panties. Things suddenly shot to super-heated, scorching.

Until they didn't.

Like usual, he turned as frosty as a snowman in a blizzard and backed away.

For a split second, she could have sworn he'd been about to cross — no, obliterate — a boundary. It had to have been in her imagination. People often remembered past events in skewed, unrealistic, exaggerated ways, going by her dealings with clients and her own experience.

After the almost-kiss, she hadn't seen or spoken with him. Years had passed, and she had no idea how he looked, who he even was anymore. She should feel neutral, relaxed, confident seeing him.

She didn't.

If only rational thought overrode emotions.

Lingering feelings swirled around her heart. There had always been something about the infuriating man that sparked like kindling in her blood.

Sage swung her hair over her shoulder. Her resigned tell, according to her supervisor. "Fine. Give me his contact info, and I'll arrange to drop by. But just so you know, I can listen and refer him on, but I can't treat him. It goes against the Australian Psychological Society's Code of Ethics."

Her brother's grin stretched over his face. She almost expected him to fist-pump the air, like he did when he told her about a winning case. Chase grabbed his mobile out of his trouser pocket and started text messaging.

Sage's phone buzzed, Alexander's address and phone number flashing big and bold on the screen. "Received."

Her brother jumped up and wrapped her in a grateful hug. "You don't know how much this means to me."

"I think I do, and you owe me at least twelve months of wine and a selection of gourmet cheeses."

He pulled back, his facial expression shocked, incredulous. "What? Twelve months! You have to be kidding. That's milking it, big time. He's my best friend, but you know him, too. And you're a great person, a selfless person, who loves helping others, so —"

She raised her hand. "Stop right there." He forgot she was also well versed in his conflict-resolution, some might say guilt-inducing, coercion strategies. "Point taken. I'll settle for a case of wine with a mix of sparkling rosé, shiraz and fortified. "And a quarterly supply of Romano, gorgonzola and smoked goat's cheese." She would not compromise any further. Even if he did the 'cute-come-on-sis-puppy-eye-pleading' thing, something he'd mastered that usually won her over.

Chase's charming smile lifted the corners of his lips. It hadn't worked on her for ages — however, she could see how his Chris Hemsworth vibe and expertise at reading people could suck in the ladies. Men, too.

As a high-end solicitor, he used a more hardball rather than therapeutic approach. He had to play those involved, negotiate, have a solid poker face, know when to fight his battles and when to cut his losses.

He would have determined reasonably quickly that he'd pushed her as hard as he could. Push her too far and she'd retreat. "Got it." He saluted her. "I'll leave you to" — he waved his hands above her desk — "this."

Chase left her office, and she stared at Alexander's details on her mobile phone. She debated whether to call or text. Given her phone phobia and 'Alexander anxiety', she decided to text.

Normally she'd have her personal assistant follow up, but this was off the books…purely personal. Assisting an old friend… Well, a not-that-old, sexy, off-limits, totally unreciprocated friend of her brother's.

She sent Alexander an SMS, put her phone on the desk and, not even a minute later, it buzzed.

What now? Another unnerving message? Another veiled threat to her life? Something she'd almost thought she'd become desensitized to.

Until it happened again.

And again.

And again.

Working in the psychological trauma field, she expected angry, unhappy patients, but this one in particular liked to taunt. They hadn't hinted at any specific danger yet, so she'd let it go.

Sage had her suspicions about possible suspects, though hadn't taken action. Her clients were troubled, which was why they saw her in the first place. She didn't want to exacerbate their issues by possible false accusations. She didn't want them hassled prematurely by the police.

Otherwise they'd lose what little trust she'd been able to gain. And that would ruin the rest of their therapy, prevent them from ever moving forward positively, putting their faith in another professional, taking the risk on another psychologist, taking a risk on themselves and their decision-making.

She swiped her mobile screen. Like she didn't already have enough on her more-than-full plate.

Alexander. Relief flooded her veins while her heart thudded like a gong in her chest.

Sage, hi. Long time no communicado. Thanks for making contact. I wasn't sure you would. When are you free? I'm at your disposal.

Her breath hitched. Why did that sound so sexy? Almost flirty. He obviously hadn't meant it how she'd read it. She had to keep her response clear, simple, to the point. No ambiguity.

Tonight at around 6 p.m. or tomorrow mid-morning.

Tonight. Please. My address is…

Tonight? She'd thought it'd be too short notice. She'd expected to have more time to get herself together…her feelings, her readiness. Maybe Chase was right. Maybe Alexander's situation needed more attention than either of them had anticipated.

Fine. See you soon.

Images of him popped into her mind. As a nineteen-year-old he'd been tall and lean and strapping…a true fitness fanatic. And those eyes… She could never forget their deep blue intensity, like a lagoon in paradise. His gaze alone had her fighting an inevitable blush.

Thankfully, her olive skin had helped hide her reaction. If he'd realized she'd had such an all-encompassing crush on him, she'd have been mortified.

But now, with his years of experience in the world, would he notice? If not through her skin tone, through her body language? See through the subtleties of her highly developed mask, her measured responses?

And how about him? Would the clichéd windows to his soul show his pain? Would he have that lost stare in his eyes? The one she'd seen so many times — a mixture of grief, loss, despair…helplessness.

Reintegrating ex-service men and women into civilian life posed a significant challenge. Their bodies and brains had become addicted to the adrenaline rush, the anxiety of combat, and struggled to cope with the mundane every day, how they fit into society.

From what her brother had said, Alexander seemed affected by the usual PTSD symptoms — unrelenting nightmares, persistent flashbacks, disassociation from reality. She prided herself on providing sessions that explained the phenomenon in a caring, sensitive way and engaging clients in effective, evidence-based treatment.

Sage couldn't get involved with Alexander, though — not personally, not professionally. She'd have to give him impartial advice and refer him to a service that could objectively explore his situation in more depth.

From her interventions with clients, she'd learned they often required a healthy reset, some time to readjust. It reinforced that soldiers needed a therapist who wasn't conflicted and space to readapt, a skill they knew well.

Having chatted with a range of veterans, she understood that in a war zone they quickly and efficiently reacted in order to save others' lives in addition to their own. Could she help Alexander, too?

At least put him on the right path without getting too entangled?

Positive change could take its toll. It wasn't enough for some veterans to be out of immediate danger. Many times her clients experienced recurring night terrors that brought them right back to the scariest, most guilt-and-remorse-ridden situations of their lives.

And it felt real, almost tangible. They described the explosive sounds, the smoky smell, the metallic taste. A high percentage of her patients relived it daily. Forget all the other complications. It fucked with a person's psyche, their state of mind, their self-worth. Everyone needed time to reacclimatize.

In her case, with Alexander, she didn't have as much preparation time as she'd prefer. And she had no idea how long she'd need. Most likely she'd never be entirely ready. Given their text-exchange agreement, she only had a few short hours to psych herself up.

Would he continue to see her as Chase's annoying little sister? An irritating, yet possibly helpful hassle he had to deal with on top of his emotional, mental and probable physical scarring? Or would he take her suggestions onboard, her advice, acknowledging her professional expertise?

Did it even matter? She'd do her best and hope he got something out of their informal chat. Then, if he found it useful, she'd suggest a referral to an external, unbiased professional. Knowing him, even a little, could cause a competing interest. Her damn irrational emotions had already been triggered.

The best advice came from an unprejudiced place, hence why he needed someone independent, someone unbiased to provide intervention in the longer term. If she got him to understand that, she'd consider the interaction successful. Professionally, anyway.

Sage leaned into her office chair, closed her eyes and blew out a long, centering breath. She could do this. Like her brother said, she loved helping. So why should Alexander be any different?

Because he always would be, had always been special. Branded himself on her soul...irreplaceable, irremovable, permanent.

A familiar ding announced she had a new email. She snapped her eyes open and —

Not again. Goosebumps prickled along her skin.

Her heart galloped and her mind went AWOL.

The message frequency continued to escalate — sometimes email, sometimes text, sometimes social media. *Not a good sign.*

No. She shouldn't jump to fear-based conclusions.

Not yet. Before she went to the police, she needed more concrete evidence to prove she was in jeopardy or else they'd laugh her out of the station.

Getting a reputation as a jumpy, neurotic, hypersensitive psychologist wouldn't help her business.

The newest unsettling message sat at the top of her inbox and practically glared at her. The same email address as all the others. Some generic thing that undoubtedly couldn't be traced.

The title drew her eyes to it like a magnet.

Time is running out...

Curiosity got the better of her over-vigilant mind, and she clicked into the body of the email.

You'll soon get what you deserve.

Dread burned her stomach as though she'd sculled a double shot of cyanide. Like the other posts, it wasn't an overt threat. It could be interpreted any number of ways. And she refused to play into this person's game. Whoever had instigated this attack obviously hoped it'd put her on edge, unnerve her, make her fearful. Fuck her up.

And yes, okay, it did. It had…somewhat. She tried not to be the last to leave the office, made sure daylight still hung in the sky, warily checked the car park and held her keys in her hand like a makeshift knuckle duster.

Sage knew all about the power of paranoia, had seen it countless times in her therapy sessions — how it insidiously took over her clients' lives. She wouldn't allow that to happen to her. Her profession should make her immune. Right? She understood how it worked.

Rather than block the sender, she moved the email into a separate 'Threats' folder in case she needed evidence later. She'd also kept all the text messages and private-messenger social-media posts as a backup.

Over the years she'd heard too many stories of disgruntled patients attacking their therapists. Hopefully it wouldn't get to that. However, it paid to be cautious.

About the Author

Sandra Carmel is an Australian author of racy, flirty and downright-dirty romance novels, novellas, short stories and poetry, who enjoys stimulating herself and others with words. An obsession with classic romance novels, particularly Jane Eyre, and her infatuation with Mr Rochester were key motivators in commencing her romance writing journey. So far, she has taken the scenic route from steamy paranormal to sci-fi to contemporary, creating provocative stories that delve beneath the surface of desire. She reads and writes a lot, frequently disrupted by her ever-attentive, cheeky cats, and sinfully amorous array of book boyfriends.

Sandra loves to hear from readers. You can find her contact information, website details and author profile page at https://www.totallybound.com

Home of Erotic Romance

Sign up for our newsletter and find out about all our romance book releases, eBook sales and promotions, sneak peeks and FREE romance books!

www.ingramcontent.com/pod-product-compliance
Lightning Source LLC
Chambersburg PA
CBHW050523260626
47157CB00004B/1442